DEAD MAN'S
SWITCH

By
Liam Sweeny

JOYRIDE PRESS

Published by Joyride Press

69 Heartt Avenue, Apt. 2
Cohoes, NY 12047

ISBN-13: 978-0-9897014-9-5

Books have led some to learning and others to madness.

Petrarch

Sawdust

The grey, rotted wood splintered and cracked beneath their feet as they walked the North Pier. It used to be full of hustle and bustle and bullshit spoken by bourbon-drinking poker players on the ground floors of the many bordellos that silhouetted the night sky, now as broken as the pier. Things weren't what they used to be.

Flip James adjusted his fedora before tucking his rough hands into the pockets of his overcoat. He wasn't always a venture capitalist. He used to work in a steel mill outside of town. He still had scars on his wrists from the searing heat of stray sparks. It was work to him, not the *American Industrial Dream* that people romanticized it to be. He'd come home dirty, smelly to a nagging wife and a six-pack of Miller High Life. That was the closest thing he had to a *High Life* back then. He was a beer-drinking, cigarette-smoking lotto-player. It was that last thing that changed his life.

He won, and he won big. Thirteen million, which was huge back then. He blacked out from the celebration, but he kept his head after the hangover went away. He invested wisely, and as of three days ago, his net worth was seven-hundred and fifty million. He made his fortune by his own name, *Flip*, flipping failing companies into profitable ones.

Which brought him here.

He loved a girl once; not his wife. He tolerated her. But he loved Betty Anne Mason. He met her on the North Pier when he was sixteen. There was an amusement park back then, long ago dismantled for scrap metal. He wrote her love poems, and she wrote him back. They spent hours on the beach, looking up at the stars. He even bought a book of the constellations at the town bookstore, studied it to impress her. She was beautiful.

On his eighteenth birthday, he'd finally saved enough money, even sacrificed getting his own car to buy a two-carat diamond ring for her. He was going to propose as he made his way to the North Pier. He turned the corner to see her lips locked with Spencer Richards, the town's rich kid, off to Princeton that year.

In a letter, she told him that she cared about him, but Spencer could offer her a way out of that shitty little town. She wanted the best for herself. They were married as soon as he finished school. Flip was invited. He put in for overtime that day.

"Flip, I can't believe you're considering buying this place." Jonas Gilmore, his financial advisor said as they stood out on the pier, getting swept by the cold ocean breeze.

"Bought it. Not considering." Flip said.

"Well," Jonas struck a match to his pipe, "what are you gonna' turn it into?"

Flip looked back one more time at the place filled with every truly memorable moment in his young life; his greatest hopes, his darkest fears, most vivid pain. He turned back to face the ocean.

"Sawdust."

Tough Times

A Phoenix Tale

Red, white and blue neon streaked across the bar from the sign in the front window of the Phoenix Hotel lounge. Sam Morrow slumped over his fourth vodka, drowning the din of the joint. He set his weary eyes on Walter, the leathery bartender, who was chatting up a pouty julep at the opposite end.

Sam scoped the lounge, eyeing the pool-table in the center of the checkerboard floor. Breaking pool balls collided under the unforgiving pulse of overhead fluorescents, catching the room's thick hazy smoke as it hung over the pock-marked green felt. *C'mon, Walter,* he thought, *C'mon, C'mon, C'MON!* He backwashed the vodka, mindful not to kill it too fast.

Glass already half-empty; he'd need a refill soon. He pulled the billfold out of his back pocket, thumbing a fifty to square up and re-up. Maybe the flash of cash would pull Walter out of the dame's orbit.

As he waited, he pulled a 2x3 full-color glossy from the picture-flap; Janice and the kids. He remembered arguing with her over the pics the day they had them done. E.G Laurel's, the most expensive photographer in town, booked to a three month waiting list. Sam heard Laurel had to close shop last month.

He cocked his head to the left, stared at Janice's face as the light shimmered off it. She was flushed with vitality back then, punch-drunk on the comfortable life they'd led. Tommy, Aaron and Chrissie were just kids, overjoyed that Laurel had a doll that made fart sounds. All teenagers now; he and Janice could see retirement in the horizon.

Life was funny.

In easier times, he had a nice house, two cars in the garage and a small racing boat, none paid for. Over the past year he watched as, one by one, everything he had was repossessed, down to his vows. Two weeks before, Janice asked for divorce.

Sam tucked the picture back in his billfold. He was raised to be an honorable man, and he couldn't help but feel nauseated at where he was, what he was about to do. But honor was a rocky road.

Liquid gurgles snapped him back to attention. He looked up to see Walter refreshing his vodka. The fifty lay untouched.

"On the house, Sammy," Walter pushed it back. He tapped on the bar, making the shape of a gun with his fingers, subtly pointing them to the back booths. Sam's gaze followed his index finger.

"That's him," Walter said. "Better get over there; he don't stay long."

Sam patted him on the shoulder as he got up.

"Thanks, bud," he said. "And thanks for the hook-up." Walter nodded.

He walked past the pool table and the jukebox; *The Final Countdown*, by Europe. Sam laughed to himself, the sights and sounds of pool-sharking ricocheted through his vodka-rattled mind.

The back booths were shady, single overhead bulbs encased in dusty fixtures; he'd heard they were real Tiffany glass. Sam could only make out shadows beneath the brim of the man's Panama hat.

Without looking up, the man pointed a walking stick to the other side of the booth. As Sam slid over the red naugahyde padding, he could see the man's white cashmere blazer, powder-blue satin handkerchief tucked in a three-point fold in his breast pocket. A fat cigar smoldered in the ashtray, its acrid smoke further enshrining the man's face in anonymity.

Maybe it was better that way.

"Our friend says you have a problem."

"Yeah," Sam eyed the room as he scratched at his collar. He reached into his pocket and felt the tip of the walking stick pinning his hand to his chest.

"It's O.K.," said Sam, "It's just--"

"I know what it is," The man had a calm, road-kill voice that reminded Sam of Johnny Cash. "And when we're done with our little chat, you'll leave it under the table. Are we clear?"

"Y-yes sir," Sam quickly took his hand out of his coat, "Sorry."

"It's alright," the man said, "These types of arrangements aren't ever easy."

"No, they're not." The man picked up the cigar, puffing deeply. The smoke hung on him like fog on the morning grass.

"You love her?"

"She's my heart and soul.." Sam looked away.

"Do you want it to look like an accident?"

"It can't look like a suicide."

"I see." The man swirled his drink slowly. "You do know this kind of thing will be investigated, don't you?"

"Look, if you can make it look like an accident, do it." Sam said. "But it's gotta be soon. Things are going south real fast."

"It can be done tonight," He waved his hand about to dispel smoke, "It's up to you."

Sam gazed around the bar at all the drunks, personalities soaked in alcohol, laughing and carrying on in a place that could hide the scars of tough times like cheap makeup. It was a sanctuary, rising at dusk from the ashes of the dawn.

"Tonight'll be fine." Sam's gaze returned to the shadow of the man's face. The man smiled. Sam couldn't see his face, but he just *knew.*

"How much did you bring?" He said. "*Don't* take it out. Just tell me how much is in there."

"Five, five thousand,"

"Good." He picked up his cigar, and his drink. "Finish your drink, and let the envelope fall between your legs." He said. "Kick it to the back of the booth, and go upstairs. Room 27 will be reserved for you."

"Okay," Sam replied. "Thanks, Mr.-"

"That'll do," the man said. "Mr." Then he walked to the bar.

Sam finished his drink with trembling fingers, his nostrils filled with the lingering odor of the man's cigar. He felt the urge to talk some more, but every word had been said. Now all Sam needed to do was to let the envelope drop between his legs. He tilted his glass one last time and let it fall. It felt as if his soul was freed, all-in on a half-million life insurance pot. He left the booth, depositing the empty glass on the edge of the bar. Then he staggered to the elevator.

***

The red and blue pulses of cruisers and fire trucks spiked the pre-dawn. Officer Todd Davis was called to the scene of a hotel fire. He arrived to see a black body-bag being toted out the front door. The dark streak of soot showed the intensity of the fire that had by then been put out.

"He had a cigar," the bartender told him, "He was pretty drunk when he went up,"

"Did you know the guy?"

The bartender shrugged. "He came in once in a while. We didn't talk much."

"Do you know his name?"

"Yeah, Sam," he said, "Sam..Morrow, I think."

"Does he have a family?" Behind them the City Coroner loaded the body in the meat-wagon.

"Yeah," the bartender said, "He said something about a wife once."

The cop and the bartender stood outside the Phoenix as the ambulance sped off.

"Strange," the cop said, "Third time we've had to pull a stiff outta' here this month.."

The bartender scratched his chin.

"Tough times," he said, "tough times."

The Mistake

Georgia sat in the waiting room of her OB-GYN. She was six-months along, and so far everything was good. She was thankful; she and Todd had to use in-vitro fertilization to conceive, and she'd heard more than her share of horror stories about IVF, some told by people who actually knew what they were talking about. But in her case, everything was as good as it got.

There was an old fat-back television on a tall bookcase in the corner. The news was on, as could be expected. Paul Deligard was going to be executed that day. He had kidnapped, beat, tortured and mutilated over sixty women in the Metro area over a span of two years. No one slept, not women anyway. His highlight was putting a partially dissected woman's remains on the front steps of City Hall around Christmas of last year. It proved his undoing; they caught him because he left evidence.

He plead guilty, waiving his appeals. As some kind of sick joke, he got married two months ago.

Whoever would marry him deserved to be locked up too, she thought.

Dr. Brennan motioned for Georgia to come inside. He didn't have a good look on his face. He had called her last night, which made her nervous. Now, she was even more so.

She followed him into the room and went to sit on the table, but Dr. Brennan asked her to sit in a chair.

"Is there something wrong with the twins?" She asked. He wouldn't look her in the eye. Something was wrong.

"The twins are fine, don't worry about that.." he said. "I don't need to examine you; I need to talk to you. There been a mistake."

"Mistake?" She asked, "About what?"

"I just heard from the IVF clinic," he said. "You and Todd wanted an open donor, so you would know who the father was, in case he had any medical problems."

"Yeah, Keith Benson. We've met him."

Dr. Brennan was quiet. He held a chart up to his face. She couldn't even guess the expression behind it.

"I'm not going to dance around this," He rubbed his chin. "The donor information and the vials of donated sperm are matched by a number. Keith's sperm had a twelve digit number that was assigned to it. But his sperm wasn't put into your egg. A technician misidentified the vial by one number."

"So someone else's sperm was put into me, you're saying."

"Yes." Dr. Brennan was rubbing his head bald, as it was growing sparse up front to begin with.

"So, who is he?" Georgia was pissed, but if the donor was okay medically, she'd forgive the mistake.

"The man is dying, and he donated the sperm so that his wife could conceive."

"Wait, he's dying? What does he have? How long does he have?"

Dr. Brennan slumped in his seat, his fingertips at his temples.

"He's physically healthy." Dr. Brennan said. "And he's dying today..."

"..he's being executed."

Frankie Wanted to Kill

Frankie wanted to kill that night. In a dark room saturated with vodka and stale Garcia Vega smoke, he wiped the sweat from his brow on the front of his stained wife-beater, taking apart his .44 Magnum, cleaning it and putting it back together. The muffled sounds of the Beach Boys played in the next room. He didn't know who lived there. He chugged what was left of the vodka, and stripped off his clothes. Shower time.

He'd long ago washed the sand off him, but every now and then, he'd find some he missed. That fucking sand clung to him; like everything else he'd seen and done in Iraq. It all just clung to him. He'd spend nights scrubbing himself raw.

He brushed his teeth and combed his hair. He didn't look in the mirror. He dressed in a white cotton tee and clean boxers before returning to the room. His dress blues sat on the bed, neatly pressed. He put it on, made sure that the Silver Star was pinned just right. He tucked the .44 into a side holster after putting one bullet in the chamber. He had only one target.

Frankie enlisted in the Army in 2001, after September 11th. He was twenty-four and married. His wife, Linda, was supportive, said she'd stay true to him. What a lie that was. He got a letter from her a year before he was stop-lossed for the second time. 'I just can't do this,' she wrote. She wanted a divorce. Frank wanted Al Qaeda to stop shooting at his position. He signed the divorce papers, with too much surviving on his mind to give it much thought. In combat, you have to think when you can, and when Iraq began to stabilize, his memory caught up.

The Army trains killers. Frank became a killer in Iraq, whether he wanted to or not. He remembered being ordered to drive over kids in the road because of ambushes. He could still feel the thump of one girl's frail little body going under the truck. Killing was easy, Frank had surmised. It was easy to kill if you were a killer, but once you'd done it, you'd always be a killer. There was no turning back.

Frank left the boarding house and opened the door to his Ford F-150. He didn't have much, just a tape deck and one Johnny Cash tape. He popped it in as he turned the key and peeled out. He had one place to go before reaching his objective.

Miller's was a shit-hole bar on the outskirts of town. They served food there, but aside from chicken wings, no one ate. They had two TVs on top of the bar, usually sports games. It was where he met Linda. She was supposed to meet her friends, but she showed up at the wrong bar. Frankie was there because his friends wanted to get him out of the house. He almost didn't go. Looking back, he shouldn't have gone. But there they were, and once they met, they talked until the bar closed. They exchanged numbers, and the romance blossomed.

When Frankie was discharged, they should've realized he had something wrong with him, but they just wrote down the number of a shrink and sent him on his way. He tried to find a job, and he found one; he found many, but couldn't keep any of them. He managed to find a job working grounds at an apartment complex that he kept, but the pay was lousy, just enough to afford the room at the boarding house and keep his truck and himself going.

Frank had two Bud drafts at Miller's, knowing it would be the last time he'd see it – not where he'd be going.

He got back on the road. Linda would be in bed by now, with her new fiancée, Chuck. Frankie didn't care about Chuck. Chuck wasn't his target. As he drove the highway towards Bay View, he didn't feel nervous or anxious. He felt relieved. The killer free to exact justice. No one was shooting at him, or putting bombs on the highway. No white knuckle-ride; just Frankie and Johnny Cash singing "Folsom Prison Blues"

He got near the house and turned off the lights. He popped it into neutral and let it coast in front of her driveway. He opened and closed the door without making a sound, and made it to the door undetected. He pried open a window. Linda wasn't security conscious, and he knew she wouldn't have the alarm activated. He climbed in through the window. He knew the house; she and Chuck invited him to it when he came home, mostly out of guilt. He padded his way up the stairs, turned the corner and noticed the bedroom door was cracked open. He slithered over and pushed the door open without a squeak. Linda was in bed on the right side, Chuck on the left. Frankie turned on the light.

"What the fuck-,"

"Frankie! Oh my God!" Linda screamed.

Frankie had his gun drawn by this time, gripped at his side.

"Please, Frankie," Linda pleaded, "Put the gun down!"

"I'm afraid I can't do that." He said. He paced what little space there was in the room. He ripped the Silver Star off his blues, throwing it on the bed.

"I'm a killer now, Linda. Do you know what it's like to be a killer?"

Linda was sobbing, shaking her head no.

"When you sent me that letter in Iraq, you killed me." He screamed. "You're a killer. And now I want you to see what killers do."

Before anyone could react, Frank brought the gun from his hip and fired.

"Ashes to ashes, and dust to dust" the priest said. Frankie wasn't there to see it. At the end of the ceremony, when everyone took a flower from the coffin to remember the deceased, Linda placed Frankie's Silver Star on the lid.

I Hate Shooting the Young'uns

Earl tipped back a Pabst Blue Ribbon as he ran
a rod down the barrel of his Winchester .308. They
were hunting from the porch of Earl's tattered shack
in the middle of Hicksville, the town name, if not its
one-word description. The cemetery was across the
street. They liked to go there for some reason. Earl
and Ronnie could hunt 'em from the porch. Ellie was
playing in the sandbox, with a toddler bracelet
connected to the rust-tinged metal pipe that served
as a porch column. She was laughing and throwing
sand all around, makin' a fuss, like most kids her age
do. She was three. She was bait.

Ronnie leaned back in his rocking chair. "Slow
today..." He said.

"Ayup'... I saw two earlier, but I didn't have a
good shot. Ya' know, ya' don' wanna' be pissin' em'
off..." Earl said. He kicked open the front door with
his foot.

"Maggie! We need beer, baby."

Maggie's voice wafted through the cabin.
"Two?" She asked.

"Nah, just bring out the case," he said. "We'll have 'em drunk before they lose their cold."

Maggie popped out and tossed the case on the table between them.

"Hey! Ya' done shook up all the Blue Rib's!"

"Well, don't drink so fast, asshole."

Maggie closed the door and walked away. Earl made a back-hand motion, Ronnie let out a laugh.

"I heard that!" she said.

Earl turned back to Ronnie. "How's Sue?"

"Six months..." Ronnie said... "Gonna be hard to find baby clothes..."

"I hear ya'." Earl replied. "Gettin' hard to find ammo too. Stuckey's is runnin' low on .308... I might buy an odd-six just cause there's more ammo for it."

"You can hit pretty good with an odd-six." Ronnie said. "I got one, and a shitload of ammo in the basement. We could hunt for a year off what I got, assumin' ya' don't get sloppy drunk and shoot trees."

"Fuck yourself." Earl said. Then he squinted into the woods.

"There's one... See him?"

Ronnie looked to where Earl was pointing. "Where?"

"On the tree-line, next to the mausoleums."

Ronnie squinted. "There he is."

"That one's a man-eater." Earl said. "You can tell because he's comin' for us. The other ones hide from us."

"You're takin' it?" Ronnie said.

"Wait till he gets a little closer to the road." Earl said. "Ya' remember back in the day when you couldn't shoot across a street without the Dee-E-Cee and En-Con throwin' cuffs on ya'?"

"Yeah..." Ronnie said. "Couldn't bait either."

"Fuck those pricks." Earl said. "They ain't nowhere now..."

They watched the beast as it sniffed them out, sniffed Ellie out. It was near the main road of the cemetery. It started toward the entrance, and Earl pulled up, eye to the scope, right hand thumbing in a round and slamming the bolt. He flipped the safety, and took the *kill breath*. He fired, reloaded with the speed of a life spent on the hunt, and fired two more rounds. The beast flayed, wobbled and dropped.

Earl slapped Ronnie on the back. "Let's go get a look. Bring your bag."

They high-tailed it to the kill. Earl and Ronnie stood over the corpse, at a good distance. Ronnie had a round ready in case it got a final bit of steam. But Earl landed two head shots and a chest shot.

"Damn." He said. "Tainted meat." He pointed to the chest wound. "Formaldehyde. He must've come from the funeral parlor. Couldn't a' been dead more than a week. He's was a townie. Musta' been."

"So what, we keep the head?" Ronnie asked as he reached into his bag for the bone saw.

"Yeah, but we don't stuff it... Just keep the skull." Earl said.

"He was a young'un..." Earl added as he stared over the re-killed young man.

"I hate shootin' the young'uns...."

Dark Proposal

He loved her to death. Not his, as he stood over the bloody body of an old woman unlucky enough to sport the two-carat diamond he needed to propose. She went quick on the darkened street; rather, she went quiet. One slice across the throat, ear-to-ear gushed blood and gurgling prayers to the God she'd soon be seeing. He got her from behind, and tossed the knife in a dumpster as he took off down the alley. Blood on the gloves – He'd have to chuck them in the dumpster of the restaurant. He'd get there early. Handen Apartments was only three blocks from Gardenia's.

The old woman probably lived there. He saw her at a Bingo hall at St. Joseph's gymnasium. He stayed to tail her, playing dollar cards. The thousand-dollar jackpot wouldn't buy the band holding that rock. She slipped out, as did he. He'd complain that the lowly lit block was dangerous, if he wasn't the reason being. The wind picked up, and he hoped the garbage bags he piled on top of her wouldn't blow over. She was right next to the dumpster he dropped the knife in. He told Clara he'd kill for her, and tonight he certainly proved that.

Clara was his partner-in-crime in so many literal senses of the phrase. Snatch-n-grabs, extortion, carjacking, bank robberies. Bonnie to his Clyde, she was. As he rushed down Henching Street, he remembered the first time they met. She conned him; tried to, anyway. But he'd been around, and got the jump on her. And he would've left it there, if not for the dejected, defeated look on her face outside the supermarket, slumped over on sacks of birdfeed. He picked her up, and over the past two years, taught her everything he knew. And he fell in love.

He arrived at the dumpster in Gardenia's and tossed the gloves under a bag of stink. He walked in the front door after checking himself all over for blood.

Albert King sang the blues in the club that night, his smooth voice and crisp guitar glued together with mellow saxophone lines. *I'll Play the Blues for you – Pa..* that was the name of the song. Clara sat across the small table from him, her black satin dress bunched up her legs. The waiter, a tall, lanky fellow in an un-pressed uniform and dirty apron took our order. He ordered a porterhouse steak; she had a salmon dish. The waiter came back with wine, and we sipped, savoring the taste. It was a big night. He could feel the rock in his pocket. It felt like it weighed a pound or two. Maybe it was just his nerves.

"Since when do we do fancy?" Clara said as she set down her glass.

"You don't like it?"

She touched his arm. "No, Joe, it's great." She said. "I'm just used to drive-thrus, you know?"

Joe clasped her hand in his. "We've been on the road so long I figured we needed a decent night out."

After small talk, the meals arrived. Joe motioned Clara not to eat just yet.

"Clara," he said, "I'm not good at this, but," he gulped, "In these past two years, we've been through a lot. I taught you everything you know, and you taught me the one thing I didn't know...How to fall in love."

Clara's eyes became wide.

Joe fished out the ring. He slid from his chair to take a knee, just like in the movies he saw when he was a kid.

"I'm sorry, I don't have the box..." He held the ring up. "Clara Mae Westfield, will you marry me?"

Clara stood up and walked over. Yanking Joe up by his tie, she kissed him with more passion that either of them ever expressed to each other.

"It's about damn time." She said. "And... Yes!"

Joe slipped the ring on her finger as the patrons clapped. They sat back down, and Clara admired the ring.

"This looks just like the one my great-aunt has. Except hers has an inscription on the inside from great-uncle Gerry" She slipped it off, looking at the inside of the band. Her look was one of curiosity.

"To my Ethel, forever... Love, Gerry"

"Where did you get this?"

Joe's head hit the table.

"You didn't..." Clara's tone was ice.

"Worse than you think." Joe replied.

"What do you mean, *worse!?*"

"Look, I didn't know your great-aunt lived near here. You never talked about her."

"Did you...you know..." Clara's voice went soft, "*kill* her?"

Joe's eyes welled in tears. He nodded. He didn't care, he deserved whatever he got. What he got instead was a chuckle.

"She was a bitch." Clara said. "A loaded bitch, like millions loaded, and living in the projects like she couldn't afford to live in a good neighborhood. I'm one of three in her will"

"You're not mad?"

"Oh no.." she said. "But you better plan a hell of a wedding."

Sobriety Checkpoint

A lot of people are up in arms over sobriety checkpoints. Some of them are busybodies who can't afford to be kept in a line of cars for that extra ten minutes. Others declare it a boot stomp on their constitutional right to drive. Still others are just drunks. But they set these checkpoints up. For the drivers who do a three-point to go back, they got a cruiser to chase them too.

So it's nine-thirty at night and I'm stuck in one. But I have a secret weapon, ready to spring on the officer who comes up to the window. Yes I do, it's called 'cop camouflage'. Wanna' know what it is? Actually it's not a thing, as much as one highly specialized skill set, honed after ten years of intensive training.

Sobriety. Not a drop, ten years. I have advanced training in not getting high, or driving while tired. I have a black-belt in not texting when I drive. I once spent three weeks driving cross-country without Bluetooth. No calls, no calls at all. But not just that. Certificate in defensive driving too.

The line is moving. I can see the officers about five cars ahead. Time to make preparations. My wallet is out, and I fish for my license, registration and proof of insurance. I place them on the dash, sure to catch in the officer's flashlight. They never know if, reaching your back pocket for your papers, you're really reaching for a gun. So now I don't have to reach anywhere they can't see. Anything to set them at ease.

Line moves up, four cars now. So in my head I practice what I'm gonna' say. Officers are trained to observe people closely, but they're not trained to keep themselves cool in eighty-five degree, sticky as pancake-syrup nights like tonight wearing Kevlar. So maybe they'll be off their game a bit. I don't want any misunderstandings, heavens no.

They're going to get their share of assholes, impatient people suddenly caring about their tax dollars and the occasional drunk claiming eight beers shy of their evening soak. I'm going to get up there and be the Friendly Neighbor, maybe the Responsible Citizen. I'll make sure to ask them how they're doing. After all, they're the ones that have to stand around in this weather.

Three cars ahead now. I say fuck all of the people who are against this. If there was one of these on Route 11 three years ago, tonight, in fact, I wouldn't have had to bury Annette. I saw pictures of her car torn in two by a trucker riding with Jack Daniels. I know this because the bottle flew out his window, landed in the grass without breaking. Maybe if that bottle had broken into pieces, Annette wouldn't have, is that a bizarre thought? I've thought it before, but I tell myself it's my brain trying to make sense of the incomprehensible. I started having that thought after the sentencing. Ten-to-fifteen. He got out on parole a few weeks ago.

I guess he paid his debt to society and all, but I wanted to talk to him face-to-face. I needed some closure. Needed to put it to rest. So I drove out to California, where we lived before Gloria left me for her grief counselor. What a gig that is, I tell you. Anyway, I moved to New York, bought some land upstate and built a cabin. Not pre-fab, either; I actually built the damn thing, chainsaw to finishing nail. It isn't Bob Villa, but it kept me sober, focused. I've been on the road for four days, through the desert, through Texas and all the southern states, took 95 in Florida and flew up the coast. Can't wait to get to the peace and quiet of the camp. Plus, there's some work needs doing. There always is.

I'm next up. Lost my train of thought, sorry. They got one officer at the window, the other one walking around the car, shining his flashlight, probably looking for busted tail-lights. I'm good there too, replace them every three months, just in case. Even the little bulbs under my license plate. I roll down the window to get ready, and the balmy weather is exactly that, a balm, coating my forearm as I hang it out the window. I know I'll soon have to bring my arm back in to have my hands ten and two on the steering wheel, but really it'll be nine and three, to show my comfort level.

I pull up. The officers bounces a beam of light in the car and it catches my documentation. Good, good. No passengers, nothing in the back seat.

"Good evening, officer," I say, "How are you tonight?"

The officer dips down, shines the light in my eyes. I squint just a tad, but when I relax, he can see my corneas are angel white. I stopped at motels three times on the way home to get my solid eights.

"Good evening, sir," he says, "Have you been drinking tonight?"

"Not a drop in ten years." I say.

"Recovering?"

"Lost my daughter to a DWI," I say. "Couldn't stand the stuff after that."

"Sorry to hear that," he says, "Can I just see your license and registration? I'll get you on your way. Where you headed to?"

"My cabin, out by Hedley," I say.

"Nice spot. I fish with my kid out there on the Werneskill."

"Yeah, been there. Good pike fishin'."

The officer runs my license through a little scanner he's got on his uniform. Sweet gizmo.

"Well, you're all-" He stops. His nose is twitching as he leans down to hand me my stuff back.

"Sir, did you hit something?"

"Not that I know of," I say, and I know I didn't, but my gut knows why he asked.

"You don't smell that?" The officer keeps his head at the window, moving his nose around.

"Officer, I know I didn't hit anything-"

"Green," That's the other officer. He's behind the car now. "Tell this guy to pull over."

The officer, Green, tells me to pull over at the side of the road. Now I'm inconvenienced. Now my constitutional right to drive has been infringed. More than that, I'm fucked. I ease off the brake, and just take off.

There are red and blues behind me, giving chase. Of course there'd be. I'm flying, but the roads are curvy. I don't want to hit anyone, kill someone else's little girl. I don't want to do ten years, and I certainly don't want to wind up decomposing in a pissed-off father's trunk.

Ed Was the Lucky One

Ed was the lucky one.

It was Ed's turn to drive the getaway car that Saturday night, as Carl, in his drunken stupor so eloquently reminded him.

"Your turn motherfucker!" he slurred, "Ya' wanna play, ya' gotta pay!"

Carl's favorite saying. He was fucking crazy; Ed was surprised he'd made it as long as he had without killing anybody. Half his life he'd spent in jail, the other half he spent giving society reasons to put him there. Ed could remember when he'd first hooked up with Carl, at Joey Knight's bonfire kegger behind the old Elias Jones Elementary School playground. Everyone who was cool in those days went, and Carl was the nexus of all things illegal, which, at that age, meant drugs and alcohol. Truly he was the life of the party, the light the social moths-turned-butterflies were drawn to. Ed was one of them.

Ed had a car, a late eighties station wagon he bought from his parents with the money he'd saved.

He worked at Pizza Place, saving every dime 'til he had a thousand for his mom and three hundred for registration, insurance and a few minor fixes. He'd just turned eighteen, legal to drive by himself at night when he got a fateful call.

Not from Carl. That was another fateful call. The first call was from Pizza Place, to inform him that he was fired. Infuriated, Ed hung up the phone that day without a second thought. Then he got a call from Carl. Carl had jobs of his own.

The first one was simple. Two department stores; Carl and Joey would boost from one, and Ed would return the stuff to the other one. They never hit the same department store chain twice. But they ran out of stores. Then they started holding up gas-stations, hands thrust into the side pockets of their hoodies, holding a Zippo top up front as a mock gun barrel. They only did a couple of those; there were cameras, and they sure as hell weren't trying to get caught. Carl swore he'd never go back to jail again. Ed was young enough to believe it meant that Carl would be smart.

"We're hitting Pizza Place tonight," Carl said, "Not the one you worked at; the other one." He was referring to the one in Helmsley.

"I know people who work there too, dumbass."

"It don't matter, *dumbass*," Carl replied, "I got it all figured out. They won't even be thinkin' of you."

"Whatever..."

"Are you in?"

"Yeah, I guess..."

"Yes or no, faggot!" Carl said impatiently.

"Yes, OK?" Ed replied, "God-damnit, Carl, so fuckin' pushy."

"Seven-thirty," Carl said, "Meet us at the bonfire spot. They're havin' a party; everyone'll be shit-faced by the time we leave."

Ed was the lucky one with a getaway car pulled up behind Elias Jones, gasping as Carl pulled out a chrome-plated Desert Eagle .44 Magnum. At least that's what Carl said it was; Ed didn't know shit about guns.

"Are you out of your fuckin' mind?" Ed darted his head around, fearful of on-lookers, "You can't use *that*."

"No kidding, moron," Carl replied, "I'm just gonna' bring it; that's all."

Ed was the lucky one, young enough to believe Carl when he said the gun was just for show. He drove the getaway car to Helmsley, parking the back of the lot as Carl and Joey burst into Pizza Place, ski masks covering their faces. Ed stared at the dashboard clock, each beat of the colon making him more and more nervous. Suddenly he saw Carl and Joey running. Ed turned the ignition, and they took off as soon as Carl had his body in. In his haste, Ed slammed the half-open door against the car next to him.

"Fuck!" He said.

"Fuck it, Ed, MOVE!" Carl shouted. They took off on East Avenue, reaching Route 3, hoping they weren't seen or recognized.

Ed was the lucky one two minutes later, as the car was stopped on the side of the road. Red and blue flashing pulses, strobes of law-and-order shone through his rear-view as the cop walked up to the driver's-side window. Ed was scared to death of Carl. He looked over to see that the gun wasn't in his hand. But Carl had it; that's what mattered.

"Sir, can you please step out of the car?" The cop said. Not even a license-and-registration check. He was on to them.

Ed was trembling as he slowly opened the door. As he stepped out, the cop asked Ed to follow him back to the patrol car. It was there that he asked for Ed's license and registration. Ed wanted desperately to warn him that Carl had a gun. Carl would get them the death sentence for sure. But Ed feared

Carl, and if they wound up in the same prison, Carl would know he snitched.

Just as Ed was making up his mind to warn the cop, one shot rang out from the car. Then another shot and the sound of glass splintering. The cop drew his gun, but the car was silent. Ed poked his head up to see the rear windshield cracked, and tinted cloudy red. The cop opened the passenger door and Ed could hear the sound of Joey's body hitting the gravel shoulder.

Ed was the lucky one.

Dead Man's Switch

Darius grew up on the wrong side of the tracks his father rode tirelessly as a train conductor. Long hours; he'd come home soot-coated and sweaty, those few times he could be home. He had forearms as big as the thighs of a lesser man, six-foot-four, with dark eyes framed with darker, bushy brows. Darius rarely saw him, but his father was a good man; worked so hard to get food on the table, get his mom the microwave ovens and him the latest toys - saved enough to put him through college, state college anyway. One day, when he was seven, Darius asked his dad about the trains.

"Papa, what if you get thrown off the train?" He asked, "Does it keep goin'?"

His father laughed. "Boy, that thing's got a *dead man's switch.*"

"There's a dead man on the train?" Darius's eyes opened wide.

"No, no... it's *called* a "dead man's switch. It's in case..." He paused, "in case I get thrown off the train, or I hit my head."

"Oh." Darius said, scratching his head, "but why do they call it a 'dead man's switch'?"

"That's just what they call it." His father said. He put his arm around Darius. Their house overlooked the trainyard.

"Those trains can be so heavy, and go so fast that if ya' can't stop 'em, they can hurt a whole lot of folk." His father punched straight into the air. "So they have a switch, the *dead man's switch* that shuts them down if we fail at what we're supposed to be doing."

"But you won't fail, will ya', papa?"

"No siree'…" he said, "not on my watch."

Years later, Darius got a phone call in his dorm at SUNY Oneonta, drunk as dirt, stoned to shit. State Police. His mother and father were gunned down in that same house across from the train-yard. They caught the guy pawning his mother's gold bracelets, an anniversary gift he himself bought her with his work-study money. He had to have his roommate drive him home to identify the bracelets. They never let him see their bodies; *it was best that he not*, they said. The funeral consisted of two closed caskets.

Friends and family surrounded him during the funeral, but he was numb. He was surprised how many people came to the funeral. He expected family and a few of his friends, but the priest had a packed house as he walked the mourners through the valley of the shadow of death.

It was the guys from the railroads that came, by the droves. Such a tight bunch, each having a story about how his dad saved their skin when this piece shit the bed or that train pulled into the rail-yard at the wrong time, how his granite grip pulled many a hapless soul from being crushed between a hundred tons of coal on each end. But it was the other stuff; the times that he was there for his guys during the trying times, times like that funeral.

And they were all there for Darius, offering him so many phone numbers and twenties, fifties and hundreds "just to help get him by." It was moving, and touching but Darius couldn't feel touch, or be moved by anything through the image of mom's anniversary bracelets.

Every primal, inconceivable nightmarish creature his mind could ever conceive held him captive once the blind shock wore off. He didn't measure out his life with coffee-spoons like Prufrock, but with emaciated bottles of rotgut. Then came the trial of the man who murdered his parents.

He went to court every day of the trial sober, watched the testimony, the experts, claiming insanity, and Darius just wanted to give the court a *real* example of insanity, psychotic rage aimed at the defendant. The defendant had a name; he refused to recognize it. The man's first name was murder. His middle name was convict and his last name was lifer.

Until a technicality excluded enough evidence to hang the jury and a mistrial renamed him 'Out on Bail.'

Darius saw the man again... through the scope of a high-powered rifle. He had enough money from his inheritance to rent an office space in the building opposite the courthouse for one month, with enough left over to buy the rifle and join a gun club where an old hick taught him how to shoot a quarter at two-hundred and fifty yards.

He opened the window, backing up enough to keep the barrel inside, sighted in to dead center of the chest of the murderer, waiting patiently. The dirtbag stopped to light up a cigarette before going in to start another mistrial. Darius remembered his father punching straight into the air, could hear him say the words.. *"...if ya can't stop 'em, they can hurt a whole lot of folk..."* The justice system got thrown off the train, hit its head, failed to do what it was supposed to do.

Darius looped his finger into the trigger guard, felt the cold steel of the hair-pin. He took a breath, let it out and pulled the dead man's switch.

Club Havana

"She's got an ass I could eat off of..." Boley said as he turned the dial on the old boom box, long ago stripped of his *boom.*

"I'll give you a chance to take that back before I fire on it." I said.

Thinking over his last remark, he agreed. "I didn't mean it like that, asshole."

I laughed. "No shit... unless you're ordering a side..."

Boley punched me in the arm. We were on Bourbon Street, between Drunk and Hammered. Our destination was *Club Havana*, a spot we found through a friend, said the place was a haven for adrenaline junkies. Which is what we were.

Boley did all the extreme sports: skydiving, surfing, mountain-climbing without a rope, base-jumping, you name it. Me, I was, well, a criminal. Small stuff, no murders or carjackings, but identity thefts, criminal impersonation, bank fraud, etc. I was only one step past the law, one skip across a state or county line.

We wandered through the crowds of googly-eyed, giggling college freshman girls, guys whooping from the balconies, hands full of beads. Unlucky, mostly, as the girls weren't *that* drunk.

"Club Havana's gonna be suhWEET!" Boley said. They looked at the signs, *Tropical Isle, Jazz Funeral, Mango Mango,* and then *Club Cabaret.* Club Havana was little more than a bronze placard on the wall of a teal painted brick building, connected to the balconies above. A short man stood out front, looked blue collar, almost homeless. That, their friend said, was Carlos, the doorman.

We walked up to him, and I slid him a hundred, nodded up to the door, like our friend said. He rolled the hundred in his fingers, and nodded. We went up, and a guy on the inside opened the door, rushed us through.

We could barely see a damn thing in there. It was dark. I leaned against the wall and noticed the soundproofing. Nice touch. I was expecting underground fights, dog, chicken, human, alligator if they had it. Instead, the man handed me and Boley a pistol.

"Can you shoot one of these?" The man asked us. We both said yes.

He took us down a hallway. "First up is duelling. Who you duel; it's a random draw. It's in

the dark, so hardly anyone actually gets shot."
Hardly???

He took me to a booth; I could barely make it
out, like one of those paper-target booths in cop
shows. "This is yours," He said. "And I will take
your friend to another one. On the bottom are three
small lights; a red, the one you can see now... then
yellow, as in *get ready*... and green is fire. You
won't see the person on the other side." He grabbed
Boley. "And now I'll take you to your booth." He
walked Boley down the hall and they disappeared in
the darkness.

I sat there with my gun, felt like a Glock. Hard
to see; it really was dark. I saw the red light, and
stood up to the plate. I wanted to just duck, I mean,
all they could do was kick me out. I liked adrenaline,
but this was insane. I could get hurt. Or killed. Did
they have a medic on scene? How did that work?
But, surviving a duel was about as much a rush as
you could get, so I swallowed every ounce of sense I
had and stood up in the box.

The red light just stayed red. Forever. I couldn't
see anything but it, couldn't hear anything at all.
Just the blood rushing in my ears. All of the sudden
it turned yellow. It was duck-or-not-give-a-fuck
time, and I chose number two. I aimed into the
darkness. I kept the light in my peripheral vision,

and tightened my grip. Yellow went off for a split second, I squeezed on the trigger as green came on. I felt a searing pain in my chest, and I collapsed. I was gasping for air. I could hear a muffled shriek. I knew who it was - Boley. I hit him. I felt woozy, then numb...

Enrique walked out the front door of Club Havana. Carlos looked at him.

"They didn't duck. Neither one of 'em." He said as he lit up a smoke. "Have you ever seen that happen?"

"They dead?"

"Yeah... both of them."

Carlos looked down the street. "Can't remember the last time I had to dump..."

"I still got the hollowed-out speaker cabinets in the back." Enrique said. "We'll take care of it in the morning."

Carlos shoved his hands in his pockets. "I get paid tonight?"

Enrique gave Carlos half of the money in their wallets. "Here ya' go. Just come back tomorrow for clean-up." He said.

"We're closed tonight."

Absolution

He stared at the rainbow in the puddle as he took a deep drag from his cigarette. Even a cop goes back into happy childhood days when he sees a rainbow.

Bill was out of Route 66, about 50 miles west of Flagstaff. He had stopped at Jim's Service Station for a fill-up and a chat with his old friend.

He walked in to see Jim dead on the floor, a hole in his chest big enough to put his fist through. Sawed-off shotgun. Based on the fact that blood had just begun to stop flowing meant the perps were nearby. Shit was knocked over where Jim turned the pumps on.

He didn't call it in. Using the peel-out marks to catch their heading, he slammed the cruiser into overdrive. He caught up with them in a half-hour, and sent them into the dirt with a PIT maneuver. Out of the cruiser, Glock 17 in a firing grip, he didn't dare give them a chance to respond. Quickly they were out of the car, in cuffs and in the back of the cruiser. Flagstaff was east. He sped of east, and damn near flipped the car around, making a sharp U-turn west. Back to Jim's.

The rainbow gleamed disapprovingly. It was God's covenant to Noah that he would never destroy the earth again by flood. But also, He warned Noah not to kill another man, for men were gods, and to do so would be to destroy a part of god. Amidst the cries, he knelt down before the rainbow to pray.

"Yo, where you takin' us?" one of them said. "We ain't done nothin'!"

He sped up even faster, ignoring them.

"I got rights, man!" The other one said. "I want a lawyer!"

Bill smiled. "I'm a lawyer."

"No, you're a cop."

"...and a lawyer," he said, "and in my legal opinion, you two are fucked."

"Where you takin' us?" the first guy repeated, a wiry dingy mess with jailhouse ink bleeding down his arms. The agitation was becoming fear.

"To a higher court," he said.

The wiry guy looked to the other one. "Yo, this pig's crazy!"

He pulled into Jim's. He let the two thugs out, and undid one handcuff on each, securing the free one to a solid iron bar that ran between the pumps. He walked back into the service station. He forgot one thing; he knelt beside Jim's corpse and, with his index finger and his thumb, closed his buddy's eyes, taking the sweaty rag out of Jim's back pocket. He had no family; no one would miss it. Then he looked at the pump controls again. They forgot to turn them off.

He ran through every prayer he knew, even making up a few. He looked at the rainbow; it seemed oblivious to his petitions for justice, forgiveness and grace.

He left on one pump after he left the service station, and pumped about a hundred dollars-worth of gas all over the two men, soaking the ground around the pumps. He took extra time dousing them. They resisted furiously at first, then they started inhaling the vapors, and before long they passed out. He removed the cuffs at that point.

He stared at the rainbow swirling around in the puddle of gas at his feet. He carefully unpinned his badge, tucking it in his shirt pocket. He knelt to dip Jim's rag in gasoline, and stepped back from the pump toward his cruiser. He used his Zippo to ignite the rag, and threw it into the puddle.

Flame soon surrounded the pumps, and immolated the perps as he sped off east. He drove for a few miles before pulling off in a patch of empty desert. He took his badge out of his pocket, and re-pinned it. When he heard the explosion, he hopped on the radio.

"Officer Gonzalez requesting back-up for a possible explosion, fifty miles west on 66."

The Bottle & the Cloth

A Phoenix Tale

November, 1976

"Don't ever get old, Wally,"

Bucky Roscoe spoke through carbonated gasps. It was a Saturday night, the thirteenth of November. A tradition for the past ten years, old Bucky Rogers would spend all night at the corner of the bar under the television, drinking cheap beer and unloading the year's sins like tears on Walter's shoulder. He never came to the bar empty-handed.

Bucky owned a string of New York night-clubs in the thirties; opened the first one the day FDR repealed prohibition. Bucky lived the life; saw it all, and did more than half of it. He had a string of kids, only knew two of them. They found him, he didn't go looking. They had to meet that half of their DNA. They wrote that half off shortly after spending a couple hours with him. He had that effect on people.

Bucky and Walter met at Walter's previous gig down the street. He had the same shtick then, just followed Walter up the street with it. The sins used to be juicy; lately they involved short-change temper-tantrums and stolen parking spots.

"This is my last go, Wally," Walter poorly tolerated *Wally.* Bucky, he let it go.

"You said that last year."

"But this year I got *the big ole' C.*"

Walter put down the glass he was drying. "I'm sorry to hear that, Bucky."

"Doc says it's all over," Bucky pointed to his chest, "Says I got six months."

Walter was silent. He didn't know what to say. Bucky pulled out a prescription bottle, held it up to the light.

"Doc says I can't drink on these. Fuck him."

"Did you take them already?"

"Doubled the dose, yessir," Bucky said, "Don't worry, Wally: I loaded up on Captain Morgan before I left the house. So don't hold the tap."

He pushed forward his empty glass. Walter filled it, looked in every direction but Bucky's."

"So you mean to die in my bar, is that it?"

Bucky ignored Walter, looked around the lounge. "Hey Wally, I got one for ya'. One I been holdin' back for just this moment."

"Ya' got what for me?"

"A sin," Bucky said, "A good one. Well, a *bad* one."

Walter sighed, leaned over the bar. "Go ahead Bucky."

Bucky checked the lounge again, his movements jerky from the liquor, the pills.

"I killed a guy."

"Ya' did, did ya'?"

"I'm fuckin' serious, ya' putz!" Bucky slapped the bar. Then he leaned in.

"Sorry Buck', go ahead."

Bucky pointed a finger straight ahead. His bloodshot eyes fluttered, then came to rest.

"1942," he said, "I just opened the Hopper, and the Madison Club had a record year in the tills, ya' know?" Bucky took a swig. "Lotta' young guys getting' ready to go to war trying to catch some *bon voyage* tail. Place was beautiful."

"One night this dame comes into the place; man, Wally, she was gorgeous. What I wouldn't give to have her, but she had her hooks into one of the sailor-boys. A regular, as far as regulars went. She became one too, a *regular.*"

Bucky cleared his throat. "Next night she came in with the biggest rock I'd ever seen, and I was pullin' green then. Turned out sailor-boy came from

New York social royalty. They had plans to get married when he got back from the war."

Walter listened patiently, thankful the bar was dead that night.

"He had a cushy job on an aircraft carrier," Bucky continued, "The marriage was all but a sure thing."

"Did you love her?"

"Yeah, sure; whatever passed for it in those days," Bucky said, "But I didn't kill him for love."

"How'd you do it?"

"He always drank a fancy brand of vodka, no one else would order it; too expensive. One night he'd had a few; I filled the bottle with rubbing alcohol. He died after he left – it was a page-five story in the society rag."

"Did they suspect you?"

"Kids drank themselves to death all the time back then. It was ruled *accidental.*"

Bucky took a deep swig of his beer. He swayed back and forth. Bucky Roscoe was going to die that night, probably fall right off the bar-stool. He hiccupped. Walter had to get him talking again.

"So what did you kill him for," he asked, "if not love?"

"Oh, I don't know; I was young, successful, hittin' the top of my game. But it was built on sweat and work," he said. "That kid had it all, man, *born with it;* spent years wondering whether it was the girl or the *rock* that made me do it."

"I see." Walter mulled over Bucky's confessional. Bucky mulled over his beer.

"Wally, I ain't been down the street in a while, but I need a favor.."

"And what's that?"

"Give me the Last Rites."

Walter rubbed the back of his balding head. ""Jesus, Bucky, I haven't been a priest since I left Saint Mike's."

"Once a priest, always a priest," Bucky said, "C'mon, Wally, you're all I got in the God department."

Walter fidgeted, picked up a dry glass and wiped it anyway.

"C'mon, pal.." Bucky swayed with the smoke in the air. Walter darted his eyes around the lounge.

"Fine, Buck'." He said. "I have a Bible and some oil downstairs. Let me go get 'em."

Bucky laughed. "And you said you weren't a priest no more.."

Walter went down to the basement, to a small fire-proof safe. The Phoenix Hotel kept all their valuables in it, including a Bible that had been used by the Masonic lodge that occupied the second floor in the 1790's. Why it was still there, no one knew. It was worn and dusty, but it was purely symbolic; Walter knew the Sacrament.

When he got back upstairs, Bucky was slumped over the bar. He called his name a couple of times, no luck. He pressed his two fingers to Bucky's neck: no pulse. A hand in front of his mouth: no breath. Walter told the barmaid to call an ambulance. Then he rested Bucky's lifeless head to the side.

"*Through this holy anointing*," Walter whispered, forming a cross with olive oil on Bucky's forehead, "*May the Lord in His love and mercy help you in the Grace of the Holy Spirit.*"

Walter anointed Bucky's palms. *Better late than never,* he thought.

The First

Joe Freer always wanted to be the first at everything. This was no small order in an experimental physics lab. But I always had him beat, even if only by a hair. I discovered vacuum energy first; I built the quantum array first; designed a working carrier first, and was dead-set to be the first human to ever travel time.

I was told not to do it by my colleagues. They said it was untested, and the risks were too great. *Nonsense,* I'd reply, Joe Freer knew as much about time travel as I did; if something happened, he could take over the project. I was so focused in being the first time-traveler that I was willing to risk my life for it. Never mind that I had a wife, never mind that the chances of survival were, by default, fifty-fifty; it would either work, or it wouldn't. But then I caught wind of an email chat-log between Joe and my wife. It started out with him trying to calm her down and ended with him trying to get up her skirt. He was betting on it *not* working. When I got back, I would beat the bloody hell out of him.

Then one day, about three weeks from launch, a doctor was in the control room. Joe had the day off. Doc had a plastic box full of needles. Hated them. Needles, that is. But it didn't matter. Lieutenant Colonel Gardner, the man with the money on our project, asked me to *suck it up*, for lack of a better term. They pulled a vial of blood from my arm and threw a taped puff of gauze on the hole.

"Mind telling me what that was for?"

Gardner took a picture out of his pocket. "This is to be shared with *no one*, do you hear me?" I nodded. He passed me the picture.

"We got reports this morning of a crash out in Nevada. Thankfully it was NORAD reporting," he said. "That-" He pointed into the lab at our carrier machine. "..works, apparently."

I looked at the picture. "It's a wreck."

Gardner took the picture back. "It hit the ground at Mach two," he said. "We're lucky it isn't dust."

"Was anyone in it?"

"Well, we found a body, but it was so badly mangled that we need to use DNA to determine who it is. We're collecting yours, because you're deciding to go on this flight."

"What if we don't send it?"

"Apparently we do," Gardner said, "or else it wouldn't have landed."

"Have you told Joe?"

"No.. not yet."

"Then don't," I said. "I need time to think about this."

Over the weeks running up to the launch, I thought long and hard about it: the mission, Joe's fight to be first, his flirtation with my wife. All of these things I kept to myself. I needed to know one thing first and only time would tell. And the Tuesday before the flight, it spoke.

"It's not you." Gardner said.

"Not me?"

"The DNA's not a match."

"I'm not the one who goes first."

Gardner folded his arms. "Nope'"

"It's gotta' be Joe then. He's been biting at me to send him. He's obsessed about being the first time traveler."

"You'll be sending him to his death," Gardner said. "He doesn't have the clearance to know what we know."

"I'm gonna' try to talk him out of it, without letting on."

Gardner let out a grunt. "Good luck on that."

Joe was out in the lab, polishing up the carrier. How lovingly he cleaned it. In his heart he must've known I'd send him first. He thought I didn't have the balls.

"Joe," I said, "Gardner won't let me go. You're up."

"You're shittin' me," Joe said. "Gardner was going to let you go a couple weeks ago."

"He changed his mind." I tried to hide what I knew.

"No, you're just chicken-shit." Joe laughed. "It's easy to be in a lab, but when it's time to show your sack, it just shrivels."

"You're going to die, Joe."

"I'll take my chances." Joe said as he hopped into the carrier to feel it out. "But either way, I'll be the first."

In the minutes before the launch that day, Joe tapped my shoulder.

"The scientists never get remembered," Joe said, "Just the explorers. Remember *that*."

The time-machine launch took off without a hitch, in brilliant flashing light and waves that washed over the scientists and engineers involved. The next day, Joe was given a common funeral. No fanfare, no twenty-one-gun-salute, and not once in the eulogy was his time traveling mentioned. His tombstone had just his name, his rank and his birth- and death dates.

The time travel project was above top-secret. In the real world, it didn't exist. In his race to be first in the history books, Joe Freer must've forgotten that part.

A Debt and a Dinner Plate

The curb was lined with beige and white cigarette butts, full flavors and lights desegregated. The rain pelted the neon eye-catchers and the crowds, ending its journey in gutters and streams that followed the curbs.

Jim didn't want to be there. His fedora was waterproof; so was his coat, but the chill followed the rain, strengthening his own chill over the whole mess. He walked over to the side wall of Mango Paradise. He fished for a Benson & Hedges and his Zippo out of the inside coat pocket of his jacket and sparked up.

Quick Eddie wasn't quick enough. He had a simple job – get in, get Corsivo's books and get out. He'd done it a thousand times before. But he caught a whiff of Janice Graine, Corsivo's side-girl. So the fucker makes it a social call. Corsivo caught him zipping up; Eddie was lucky to get out alive.

But now there was a debt. Corsivo wants Eddie's nuts in a jar and his heart on a dinner plate. But the boss has a soft spot for Eddie, and little love for Corsivo. So the arrangement was made; fifty large for Eddie's heart and nuts. And the boss sent Jim to make the deal.

Jim exhaled through his nose; smoke came out in dual exhaust. His job was so much easier; his *normal* job. Not this delivery boy shit. He had a wife he didn't cheat on, even when she gave him crabs last week. He had kids he wouldn't abandon. He didn't have a clean life by far, but he did his job.

Eddie was all about the life. He wore flashy shit, drove the newest car his cuts allowed him. He didn't meet a piece of tail he could say no to, despite having his own wife. He was ballsy – probably why Corsivo wanted them in a jar.

Jim had two pouches on him, twenty-five large in each. He also had his Sig in a shoulder holster. He was supposed to meet Eddie there, and from there they'd go to meet Corviso. Eddie had to hand-deliver the cash. To make sure nothing funny happened, the boss sent Jim. Corsivo didn't respect Jim, but he knew Jim wouldn't hesitate to give him a third eye.

Eddie shows up, slack-walking his fucked-up bop, wearing a white Kangol and zipped-sweater combo with enough gold on his neck to pay the fifty large by himself.

"Jimbo!" He shouted. Jim shuddered. He fucking hated to be called *Jimbo.*

"You ready, Ed?"

"Got the cash?"

"Yeah." Jim said. "Come on." He started walking down the busy street, Eddie in tow.

"I can go pay this motherfucker, Jimbo." Eddie said. "The boss didn't have to send you.."

"When we get to his door, I'll hand you the money." Jim said. "Until then, it stays with me."

"What? You don't trust me?"

"No."

"It's not *your* ass he wants."

"From what I heard, it's not your *ass* he wants." Jim said.

"Yeah..my balls, my heart.." Eddie said. "Fuck him. Let's go spend that money at Harrah's, man!"

Jim grabbed Eddie by the sweater.

"Look." Jim said. "I'm not your *man, dude, guy*. and I'm not *Jimbo.* I could be at home, spending time with my family, but instead I have to play babysitter because you can't pull off a simple burglary without catching your dick in the window. And on top of that, the boss doesn't trust you to pay for your own life. So we do this, and you get wise. Got it?"

Eddie looked like a little kid who got yelled at for pulling his sister's pigtails.

They walked through the crowds of college kids exploring the freedom to make every bad decision on their 'to do' list. Booze peddlers hung on the counters of shit-bars lining the street, colorful plastic drinks for ten bucks guaranteed to give you the best time you won't remember. Eddie fidgeted. At his insistence, they stopped at one of the vendors and Eddie got some fire water.

Big mistake.

They kept walking, took a left on Prince Street, more an alleyway than a street. There were no lights, no stores, just dumpsters, brick facades and back doors with tiny safety glass windows. The juice hit Eddie, who started squaking.

"I can get that money now." Eddie said.

"No."

"C'mon, dude! What am I gonna' spend it on here?"

"I don't care." Jim said. "We're almost at the meet-up point."

They kept walking. Jim opened up his jacket. From what he knew, Corsivo was like him; business being business. But he wasn't going to leave himself in a bind should things went south.

Jim could see silhouettes in the distance; three of them. Two were big brawny guys, from their outlines, and one fat outline, Jim knew that to be Corviso.

Jim opened his jacket cautiously, took out the fifty large.

"Here." Jim said. "Take this."

Eddie pocketed the money, and they continued on to Corsivo and his men.

"Mr. Corsivo." Jim said.

"Jim." He didn't even give Eddie any recognition.

"Eddie has something for you." Jim said. He shoulder-checked Eddie to stand forward. Eddie fished for the money, and grabbed the pouches.

"Here's fifty thousand." Eddie's voice was weak.

"Price went up." Corsivo said.

"Wait a minute..." Jim said. He knew what the deal was, and his adrenaline spiked at the possibility of a shootout.

"He gave Janice crabs, Jim." Corviso said. "So you can see my surcharge. One-hundred large, or I get his heart and his balls."

Jim pulled out his piece and chambered around with the speed over a hundred hits gave him. Corsivo's men couldn't get the draw.

"Jim, I'm surprised at you." Corsivo said.

"You shouldn't be."

Jim turned his piece to Eddie's temple and pulled. Eddie's last thoughts landed on a dumpster as he slumped to the pavement.

"Keep the money." Jim said. He kicked Eddie's corpse.

"Hope you brought a knife.. and a dinner plate."

All I Need is a Day

Chief O'Malley and Detective Sorelli stood in the dark, stale booth behind the one-way mirror. The booth still smelled like cigarettes from back in the days when you could smoke in it. The interrogation room was wired, the tape recorder on 'record.' Jimmy sat back and took his earphone off, letting out a breath of Taco Bell.

"We only got a day with him," the Chief said through the hoarse voice of the guy that put of that smell in the air. "He's been here enough. He won't lawyer up, but if we start asking the wrong questions, he might. We gotta' get him to talk. He could bring down Richie Rich."

Richie Rich was engaged in everything from jacking freighters to the global sex trade. He got the nickname for the way he flaunted his ill-gotten gains; mansions, yachts, sports-cars; he even had diamond collars on his five Rottweilers.

"What's he lookin' at now?" Sorelli said.

"Just on what we got him for, at most, a year." The Chief said.

"OK, I can do it off that."

"Where the hell were you yesterday?" asked the Chief.

"You could say I was sealing the deal..."

"Is that why you got a shiner?" The Chief pointed to Sorelli's sore eye.

"Nah, I was fucking the cleaning lady and I slipped on the floor wax."

"Smart-ass." Chief chuckled. "Go in there. *Seal the deal...*"

Sorelli hopped out of the booth and walked into the interrogation room, his game face on, cold as a rock in Antarctica. Joey Sips' sat in the hard steel chair, his cuffed hands covered in tattoos, long goatee and bald-head rolling back and forth on his head. Sorelli'd uncuff him, but Joey'd lunge. Sorelli'd shoot, and no one would get Richie Rich.

"Joe..." He said, just standing there with his hands in his pockets. "You know what we really want..."

"Ya' ain't gettin nothin' from me, swine." Joey leaned back, as best he could, and smiled.

"We have enough to put you away for a year..."

"Shit, and that's all you got to threaten me with, bitch?" Joey said, and laughed. "I did three years in Attica, motherfucker... I'll do a year in the county standin' on my head."

"If you want to..." Sorelli said, still calm. "You were a real bully in Attica, weren't you?"

"I got by."

Sorelli laughed. "You tortured the fuck outta that kid, Ian... what's his name... Ian Braun?"

Joey took a deep breath. "Little punk. Hell yeah I did." He was proud of himself.

"I just went down to Attica yesterday, know a couple guards there, ya' know?" Sorelli said, "And I was reading your prison file. All the times you put that kid in the infirmary. Word was that you fucked him...*and* fucked his woman when you got out... that true?"

"I ain't fuck him...and that other thing wasn't on my file."

"Oh, no... Ian told me that." Sorelli commented, never losing his calm.

"Fuck that punk."

"On that thought, hold on..." Sorelli left the room, back into the booth. He could see Joey twitching with his fingers like an audience member waiting for the punch-line. The Chief leaned over as Sorelli pulled an 8 x 10 from his laptop case.

"You better be going somewhere with this..." Chief said.

"That's where I was yesterday." Sorelli replied. "And I am." He walked out of the booth and back into the interrogation room. He flapped the photo before tossing it on the table.

"Five years can change a man..." Sorelli said. "After you did that to him.. and his old lady, Ian felt like he needed protection. So he joined up with the Aryan Brotherhood. That was five years ago. They made him hit the weights, push-ups, sit-ups, taught him how to fight..."

"He didn't even want to be seen talking to me on the field. I had to get him in administration after he ordered a riot. In Sing Sing."

"Thought he was in Attica." Joey said.

"Turns out he runs the Aryan Brotherhood for the whole New York prison system now." Sorelli said. "He turned out to be a good leader, good recruiter. And he wanted you to know why he flipped you the finger in this picture."

Joey was rattled now. "Why?"

"'Cause that's what he's gonna have someone do to you every day you wind up in his prisons."

Sorelli let it sink in. Joey stared at the photo. Ian was a muscle-bound, tattooed ball of rage and hatred, and he had Joey to thank for it. He'd killed three people in Attica, and Lord knows how many deaths led a line of blood back to his kites and code words on the yard.

"But I'm going to the county." Joey said blankly.

"Well... maybe." Sorelli said.

"Maybe?"

"One year is a county bid," Sorelli said, "But if we tell the ADA we want him to recommend one year and one day, well, you know where you do *that* time..."

"Excuse me... I'll be right back." Once again Sorelli went into the booth. The Chief's jaw was as slack as Joey's. Joey was gonna' spill as soon as Sorelli walked back in there; they all knew it, even Jimmy.

"Sonofabitch!" He said, slapping Sorelli on the shoulder.

"Chief, can you call ADA Rockwell?" Sorelli asked. "He'll be prosecuting. Ask him for some help with a sentencing recommendation before I go in. We can let Joey stew for an hour."

"What do I ask him to add?"

Sorelli smirked.

"All I need is a day."

Hitch-Hiker

Smitty and D-John walked out the bodega, a little shit-hole, windows barred and filled with beer and lottery signs, neon cigarette cherry glows. They had two forties in crumpled paper bags, not even waiting to leave the store before pounding them. They walked over to the corner, past the view of the store, a new block in a new neighborhood for the same business. Smitty had the bundle, and D-John was there to enforce. Too many crazy junkies stomping the grounds. But they were always for roughing up a junkie, or robbing a nice watch, or any opportunity that came up. Like a stranger in a shiny, classic black Mercedes SUV. The guy that hopped out was a little milquetoast fuck with coke-bottle glasses. He parked in back of the lot; no cameras, no one watching out. Perfect.

"Yo, let's boost that," D-John said. "The engine's runnin'!"

"Crazy... Dude'll report that stolen quick-fast; we won't get far."

"Joey's chop' is two blocks down," D-John said. "We don't *have* to get that far."

They walked up to the SUV. It was purring. They didn't think; thinking wasn't what kept them on the block, or in a cell-block, their whole lives. They hopped into the heavy smell of air freshener, masking a much nastier smell. D-John put it in gear, and eased it back out. Joey could slice out the smell. They'd still get a couple large for the car. They sped off, Smitty catching the guy in his rear-view. Fucked up thing was, the guy just waved good-bye.

They got to the chop-shop and D-John rapped on the garage door; two, by three, by one, by four. The door slid up, and Joey walked out, bear-hugging D-John. They went to P.S. 13 together. They were tight. He motioned Smitty to drive it in.

"It stinks, Joey." D-John said, "But everything's good."

"I can smell it from here, dog." Joey grabbed a flashlight and poked his head in the front-door, unlatching the back door and unlocking the trunk. The smell became unbearable. Joey lifted a blanket off the back seat; no sooner than he did it that he turned around and puked. Then the voice came on through the stereo.

"Enter deactivation code, Mr. Barrow."

Ding!

Joey screamed at D-John. "There's fucking body parts in this car! Did you even bother to check the back seat!?"

"I-I Just thought..."

"You don't think, D-John!" Joey screamed. "You *never* think about *shit!*" Joey rubbed his temples. "Where the fuck you get this?"

"Over at the bodega, Joey...I'll just drive it back."

"Oh yeah." Joey was furious. "Leave *your* prints, *my* prints, and *my crew's* prints all over it by the time the dude you stole it from has five-o there about getting' his car stolen."

"He got *bodies* in this piece! You think he's callin' cops, Joey?"

One of his other mechanics looked in the trunk. He puked too. "Trunk's full of 'em." He said between hurls.

Ding!

"And it's got an alarm, fuck is wrong with you?" Joey said. He went to the workbench and grabbed a pair of pliers before reaching into the center console to clip the wires on the alarm. Then his eyes bulged when he saw what the alarm was wired to.

"Holy sh-,"

Ding!

***

They both felt the earth shake as the explosion rocked the neighborhood.

"What in the hell was that?" asked the clerk at the bodega.

"Sounded like a propane tank blew up."

"You want me to call your cops about the car?"

"Oh no, that wasn't my car." the man replied, pushing his coke-bottles up the bridge of his nose. "It was just a couple of strangers that dropped me off here. They picked me up on Route 43 – I had to hitch."

"Gotta' be careful 'bout hitch-hiking 'round here." The bodega clerk said. "You never know who's gonna' pick you up."

The man turned to him as he dialed 411 on his cell for a cab. "I guess I was lucky. Thank you, sir."

The bodega clerk went back inside. The wiry man dialed *3* on his phone.

"Hey," he said. "It's Barrow. It's all taken care of."

"What do I owe you?" said the voice on the phone.

Mr. Barrow could hear the whoops of the fire engines and the screams of cop cars.

"A new Mercedes," he said. "I'm heading you're way."

"How are you getting here, John? Plane? Bus?"

"I'll get there, don't worry..." Barrow said, feeling the weight of his heat in the shoulder holster. He laughed. "I might just hitch-hike."

Shiva

The club was unusually dark that night. Not even a club, really. Just a shit-hole bar with a big auditorium off to the side, a disco-ball, strobes and a DJ playing techno-music. On weekends they had what the Borderland called "raves," though a rave without ecstasy is really a bunch of kids pretending, if you ask me. The rest of the week, it was thirty- or forty-somethings dancing drunkenly to whatever classic rock music the once-had-a-shot "musicians" wanted to cover. That night even they were quieted down from normal. Everyone's eyes were glued to the overhead TVs at the bar, all on the same news-channel, reporting a local story turned international. The anchorwoman was split-screen to a video-feed of the carnage earlier that day in Glenwood, twenty miles east of Borderland. It was there that the U.S. military was able to kill the monster.

"The bombardment lasted approximately three hours." She said. "Eye-witness reports say that what looked like a nuclear weapon was employed. No body has been recovered, but General Fields assures

us that the bombardment would've pulverized it."
Shot switched to the Pentagon Press Briefing room.
General Fields was G.I. Joe incarnate, granite
features and a square jaw. He shuffled papers
around the podium before he spoke.

"As of 1200 hours Eastern Daylight Time, we
were successful in annihilating the creature that
called itself *Shiva.* We would like to note that Shiva
was a name used by the creature, but it is not to be
confused with the Hindu god Shiva.

"It started out as a human by the name of Jacob
Bell. There are many...questions we have, and that
the world has, but one question we can finally put to
rest: Is it, is he, still out there? And the answer is
no."

Cheers from the bar as the general opened up the
floor to questions.

"How can we be sure it didn't escape?" asked one
reporter. "I mean, you've bombarded it before."

"We'd recently developed an electromagnetic
trap." the general said. "Quite frankly, it had
nowhere to go."

"There have been allegations that Shiva was
originally part of a military experiment. Can you
confirm or deny this?"

The general smirked, but recovered. "We get
allegations like this all the time, about pretty much

every bad thing, but I can assure you we had nothing to do with this. We have just as many questions as you do."

"There were eyewitness reports of the use of a low-yield, or *tactical* nuclear weapon. Is this true?"

The general shifted in place. "Unfortunately, yes, this is true. The yield was small enough to produce negligible after-effects, and the threat was severe enough to outweigh the threat of deployment. There will be more about that in the President's up-coming address."

"What caused this, Jacob Bell, to become Shiva?"

"Again, we have the same questions as you all do. Honestly, we don't know."

The general took a question from the back.

"General Fields, if, hypothetically, you weren't successful in destroying Shiva, what's your back-up plan?"

"There is none." The general replied frankly. "We're confident we destroyed it this time. No more questions." The general grabbed his papers and walked out of the press-room.

Back to the anchor.

"Once again, that was General Fields's briefing on the destruction of Shiva in upstate New York," she said. "Apparently, according to what the general said, a low yield, or tactical nuclear weapon was employed in its destruction. With me are..."

The people at the bar started chattering quietly, but they were all stunned. I wasn't stunned, by any of it. I was there.

"That nuke won't hurt ya'..." I said aloud to no one, to everyone.

"How do you know?" One of the big guys in the corner asked me. The barmaid looked on. She lived near there. Maybe she's the one I said it to, who knows.

"Tactical nukes aren't designed to produce a lot of radiation or fall-out. You're doing more damage to yourself drinking and smoking one cigarette than you would if you breathed in that air down there. Besides, the wind disperses it all."

"Well the thing destroyed Shiva, didn't it?" The guy's smaller buddy said.

"Did it?"

"So you think it's still alive?" The barmaid asked.

"Don't listen to him, honey. He's full of shit."

I chuckled. "Shiva can read the minds of every human on earth, and he can enter them." I said. "Don't you think he'd know they were designing that trap, and cause one of the engineers to put in a back-door?"

The room was pin-drop after I said that.

Big-guy spoke up. "You so smug, chucklin'... What if he came here? You wouldn't be so smug if he was staring you down, huh?"

I slid a twenty on the table, looked over at big guy, Earl Watson was his name. "I'll bet you twenty that he shows up here in the next ten minutes. Whattaya' say?"

Earl got up, walked over. "You're talkin' crazy. I ain't bettin' you nothing!"

"Why not?" I said. "An easy twenty, right? He's dead, isn't he?"

"Bet him, Earl! Take his money!"

"Arright, fuck it. I'll take your bet. But if he doesn't show up here in ten minutes, get the fuck out of here and don't come back. Understood?"

"Sure thing." I ordered a beer and washed it down. At 9:45 in bet-time, Earl walked over to "escort" me out. He went to reach for my shoulder. I flung my hand out, and Earl was suspended in the air, clutching his throat. The barroom was wide-eyed. I moved my arm to the left and he crashed into the dartboard, pinned as if a thousand darts were holding him there. I hopped off the bar-stool, my black leather trench-coat opening to the swirling darkness that encompassed me. My eyes were volcanic bursts of molten red, and I floated over to the dartboard, causing a shockwave to explode every bit of glass in the bar. I hovered inches from his face.

"Pay up."

Trophies

"I really don't mind the scars," Kimmy said to Dr. Jameson.

They were in his office, long after hours. If anyone at the clinic knew he was having an affair with his patient, he'd be out of a job. His rise in his profession was atop a heap of bills, and private practice was a whole new summit of loans away.

He never meant to fall for Kimmy. She was a sixteen year-old prostitute with borderline personality. She'd had such a troubled life. His reassuring voice, the sense of security he exuded, made her feel love. His libido, maybe his egotism, made him feel lust.

But she'd attached too quickly, and he couldn't risk hurting her. She was a cutter, releasing her anguish with a buck knife. She was a worse case; facial scarring. She had five pronounced scars across her face. If her body hadn't compensated, he wouldn't have fallen for her. But the maintenance guys were talking, and he'd just told her, as gently as possible, that they had to return to a "therapeutic" relationship. She had to be told what that meant.

"Therapeutic..." Kimmy said, her gaze distant.

"Yes, therapeutic... the way we were before we became... intimate."

"But we were intimate the whole time I've been coming here."

"I mean, not sexual."

Kimmy stood up. She looked out the window. "But... I thought you loved me."

Dr. Jameson shifted in his seat. The consequences he threw to the wind when he first touched her knee, sliding his hand up her thigh as his words, so gentle, lulled her into the calm he needed to make her feel it was right; *he* was right. All the consequences – the loss of his license, his marriage, the prospect of helping rapists deal with their inner children in prisons.

He wasn't thinking of Kimmy's health. He'd done it to enough unstable patients, and it would come down to his word against hers. He had an allegation once, but he sweet-talked the stupid cops with words like "transference" and "obsessive-compulsive disorder," "borderline personality" – He wasn't bothered again. He knew how to be subtle... So far.

"I do love you," Dr. Jameson said. "but it went too far. We need to rewind–"

"You mean pretend it never happened?" Kimmy was starting to shout. She began to scratch her face.

"Kimmy, don't..."

Kimmy pulled out a knife. It was a small, three inch buck knife. She slid the side along her lips.

"Put that down, Kimmy. Please," he said as he got up. "This is not the answer..."

"So what is, Jack? I just accept one more man manipulating me for sex? Just walk out the door without showing you what it does to me?"

"Kimmy...."

"I really don't mind the scars," she said. "You must have been too busy trying to get in my pants, you never asked me why I did it."

"You're a cutter, Kimmy. I did my dissertation on cutters."

She headed for the door. Jack wanted to stop her, but he thought it might be in his own interest if she left. His career might be on the line.

She walked over to the door.

"You won't have to worry about me anymore," she said.

She grabbed the door, and locked it. Then she turned the knife on Jack.

"You thought I was a cutter. But, even though you've seen every square inch of me naked, you've only seen five scars. Did that strike you as odd?"

"Kimmy, what are you-" His words were halted by the searing pain in his gut as Kimmy stuck the knife in just above his belt-buckle. Blood gushed out, staining her hand, his pants, the floor, and he felt faint, powerless against this little girl.

She sliced him up to the sternum, unzipping his pants with her other hand and pulled the knife out. His pathetic attempts at a struggle amounted to keeping his entrails inside his body. She was careful not to pierce his lungs. She'd let him bleed out. She waited until the maintenance people left for a reason.

"I'm not a cutter, Jack."

She wiped the blood off her knife and started to slice her left cheek. She held up the cloth to catch her own blood.

"The scars, I don't mind them," she said as Jack slumped in the corner of his office, leaking crimson on his shredded white button-down.

"They're not repressed pain," she said. "They're trophies. Every time I give an abuser what's coming to him, I give myself a trophy I'll never forget."

Jonas Turley

A Phoenix Tale

Jonas Turley spent his last breath in a frayed easy chair, listening to a vacuum that reverberated with the sounds he grew up to. In the early morning hour, the north wing of the Phoenix had exhausted its revelry, hallway empty except for old Barney Ellis, a down-town drunk who squatted every night when the manager passed out. Jonas's end-table was cleared, but for the ring of dust that still held the shape of his FM radio. The pawn-ticket crinkled in his grip. The shades were drawn down to the crack of dawn as it pulled the shadow of the adjoining block across his bed. The vacuum continued to hum, eliciting a scratchy grumble from Ellis. He cursed the maid in English; she returned it in Spanish before she rapped on Jonas's door. She was a nice old woman, curses aside, always offering her garbage can to save Jonas a trip downstairs.

Or maybe she collected bottles.

Jonas had them all; domestic, Mexican, European, micro-brew—every night he'd sit in that room, traveling the world in a brown bag. Everyone knew him as the gracious, easy mannered guy with the taste for fine beer and classic Motown. He was a running catalog of Motown artists; you name them and he could roll out at least two minutes, no matter how obscure. Too bad there wasn't a job for a guy with Jonas's skill.

He had a son in his thirties, James, who stopped by the Phoenix every month to check up on him, bringing food sometimes, or toiletries. James didn't drink, but he never got on his dad about it. Jonas was absorbed in the heavy liquor through most of his kids' lives, but he never took to being physical. He was a quiet, happy drunk, but he was a drunk. The kids went without often as they grew up, and Frank and Jenny stopped visiting years ago. James was the last one left.

"Yo Jonas," an agitated voice came from the hall with a quick knock, "Lemme' in man, it's Charlie!"

Charlie tried the door handle, and it opened up. Jonas never locked his door; he was usually there. Charlie walked in and slumped down against the inside wall.

"You sleepin, Jonas?" Charlie said, not bothering to check. "..that's OK; I just gotta take hits, and the cops been up this way all day." He pulled out a glass stem and the corner of a pinched baggie that held twenty bucks of Charlie's panhandling money. Like a surgeon, he split the rock in two, stuffing one in the stem and the rest back into the baggie, back into his ratty coat. With the lighter rigged to burn hotter, he torched the rock, greedily sucking every wisp of smoke from the stem. He sucked wisps of smoke from the air like a goldfish eating flakes of food in the bowl.

"You don't know what you're missing, Jonas," Charlie said, "It's like lookin' through God's eyes." The pawn-ticket fell from Jonas's hand. Charlie scooted over to pick it up.

"Oh man, that sucks, Jonas," he said. "I'll hook you up." He took another hit, holding it in until he couldn't help but choke out. "You need some sun up in here – it's like a motherfuckin' death house."

Charlie polished off the half-rock he'd shoved in the stem.

"Suzie, that slut; she be creepin' around here." He said. "You let her in here, she'll clean you out." Charlie looked around. "..not that she'd get anything.."

Charlie put the stem in his pocket. He walked over to the window, navigating his way through beer bottles, cans and fast-food wrappers. Jonas wasn't good around the holidays – Charlie had known him for well over a decade. Come Christmas and New Year's, Jonas always shut himself in his room for the two weeks that comprised the holiday season.

"Arright, Jonas," he said, "I'll let you sleep it off." He went to pat Jonas on the shoulder, but he just made a half-motion. Then he slowly closed the door. Shortly after that, the maid did the return trip. She had a transistor radio on her cart. As she came back around, that sweet music wafted into Jonas Turley's room.

The first fly was crawling around his left nostril.

The Rogers County Weatherman

Jeb's wrist was Rogers County's best weather service. Every time Maggie Dillard and the church group wanted to plan a bake sale in the parking lot of the A&P, She'd call Jeb the day before and ask if they needed tarps and such. When Johnstown had its Flag Day parade, Mayor Owen would ring the shack and ask Jeb, "How's the wrist?" He even offered Jeb a spot on the old drop-top Caddy that the veterans rode on, but he'd never take it. He wasn't a vet, but for the war at home. The war at home was what made him a weatherman.

He absorbed the pendulum creak of the rocking chair and set his eyes on the pasture. The feed was up again this year. He had to sell a few of his cattle well below what they could've gone for, and it bit into him. Emmy was settin' to go into the third grade over at the new school building, the one they put up after the twister wiped the other one flat. The whole town had a lead heart when they pulled the bodies out – eleven got crushed in between two brick walls. Jeb had to admit to himself it wouldn't be easy to let her out of his sight. Never was.

He rubbed his wrist. Been white hot all day. Something was coming, and he had to call someone. He also had to get Emmy from the babysitter. He was a single dad. He could have watched her, but he spent all day working heavy machinery. She was an adventurer, not a good profession for a kid when chainsaws and wood-chippers are close by.

He hopped into his F150 and it came to life with a sneeze of exhaust. He took no time backing off the rutted dirt road that led up to the cabin. Everyone was at the factory, shoveling their last bit of coal ticking seconds in their head till the closing whistle. Soon they'd be home, eating steak and gravy and mashed potatoes with their wives, handing out assorted ass-whoopings to their kids, or if unblessed, nuking TV dinners and watching the shit that passed for news on their flat-screens.

Jeb drove by Johnstown Park, and much as he didn't want to, he looked at the pavilion. His wrist tingled as he brought himself back to the day he became the town's weatherman.

Mary Lou was the town's veterinarian. That's how they met. He had a sick cow, and she came over. Had Jeb been the town weatherman then, he would've told her to come by the next day, because they got hit with a bad storm, they called them *supercell* storms. Lightning and thunder and downpour like God was emptying the wash basin. The road back to town was undriveable till the next day, and Jeb offered Mary Lou a place to spend the night.

Jeb was an honorable man, from good stock. They spent the night talking, and Mary Lou dazzled him with stories of Paris and Egypt and her summers spent with her missionary parents in Chile and Peru, and her love of soft jazz. Jeb was drunk in her passion and her intense eyes. When they got married a year later, he still couldn't figure out what she saw in him.

Bliss reigned and in a year they had Emmy. Jeb and Mary Lou were county angels on pink clouds, but Mary Lou's turned red. Jeb didn't see it, like a frog in a pan of water brought slowly to a boil, he fed benefits to his doubts until he ran out of benefits. Jeb realized he represented something to Mary Lou that he didn't represent to himself. He was her prop.

Her antics got further and further out of hand, her displays of anger and jealousy more and more public. When she accused his only hired hand, Louise, the milker, of sleeping with him, that was it. Louise was seventy-three.

The divorce was a one-sided affair. Jeb got Emmy because Mary Lou's only evidence was herself, and it went south on her. But it wasn't over.

She showed up at the Southpaw, yelling about child abandonment when she knew damn well Jeb had his girlfriend Karen taking care of her. She stalked Karen too. They both got restraining orders, but the judge could barely keep a straight face when he looked at big, tall Jeb. Yet Mary Lou stayed away until the Fourth of July picnic in Johnstown Park.

Jeb and Karen were sitting with Sheriff Brown, Jeb's closest neighbor, who was off-duty.

"Jeb, I don't mean to say nothing, but I caught Emmy by the fence." He said. "I love the little girl, I just don't want her to get hurt, with the dog and all.."

"No, I agree. Thanks for lettin' me know." Jeb said. "I built a play fence for her. I guess she must've figured it out."

"That's a smart kid you got."

"Yeah. She's gonna' be a handful in a couple of years."

"I imagine she's a handful now," the Sheriff said.

"Yeah, sure is."

Sheriff Brown set upon his barbequed chicken, but something caught his eye. He got up and put his hand on Jeb's shoulder.

"Don't move," He said. "I'll take care of this."

Jeb didn't have to turn his head to know it was Mary Lou, but he did, just in time to see her slide a syringe out of her sleeve and stab the Sheriff in the shoulder with it. She hit the plunge. He grabbed onto her, holding her back some, but his grip slipped and he collapsed on the floor.

Shrieks filled the pavilion. Karen got between her and Jeb, but Mary Lou back-handed her. As Karen lost her footing, Mary Lou jumped on Jeb.

"You think you can take my daughter from me, you dumb cowshit?" Her eyes were pools of pupil. She pinned his arm to the table with her grip, which was ten-fold as strong as it should've been. She put the wrist of her other hand in front of Jeb's face. It had a horizontal slash on it, stitched together like he'd seen her do to livestock. She grabbed a serrated steak knife off the table.

"I want you to feel what I felt, honey." She smiled, eyes furious as she started slashing across his wrist, back and forth like she was cutting overcooked roast. Jeb felt the fire of adrenaline coat the blade. Then his fingers fell asleep. Then his palm, his forearm. He cried out when he saw the blood pouring from the cuts onto the white cotton tablecloth, soaking it.

By then people had pulled her off. Jeb scrambled to scrunch up the rest of the tablecloth, to keep his blood from flowing out, hell, to push some of it back in. But as the voices grew louder, the pavilion got darker.

Jeb took a year to heal from that. He regained function in his hand and arm. Not perfect function, but he only needed so much to do his work. But then he got his weatherman thing. Within two years, it was well established that his freak ex-wife made him a weatherman. He couldn't just predict rain, he could predict how much. He wasn't much good on tornadoes though. A whole lot of folk in town were angry that he couldn't give them warning, but his hand was on fire that whole day. Just like today.

Theresa, his babysitter, lived in a flat above the five-and-dime, though why they still called it that baffled him. He walked up the steps on the side to her door and saw a note taped onto it.

I took Emmy to the store. Be back soon. Come in. I have tea.

Jeb jiggled the door handle. It was unlocked. Jeb walked in to the smell of lemon herbal tea. He was a coffee man, but he figured he might be waiting. He felt the pot, and flipped the dial on the top burner. He could hear the TV in the living room, and something unnerving on the radio – soft jazz. He would've turned it off were he not a guest. He reclined on the La-Z-Boy in the living room and caught the early version of the evening news.

"Police are still investigating the accidental release of three committed patients at the Williamson Psychiatric Center." The anchor said. Jeb felt like he had passed through a cloud of fear, and had ingested some of it. Mary Lou was in there.

"Two of the patients have been found, but the third has yet to be located." The anchor continued. "This is the third time in two years that Williamson has come under criticism for-,"

Jeb turned off the TV. The sound of smooth jazz filled the room. Jeb knew Theresa was a good babysitter. He knew they sometimes went to the store.

What he didn't know... was what Theresa's handwriting looked like.

He ran room to room until he found what he didn't want to find – a huddled mass of stained sheets with two feet jutting out of one end and Theresa's auburn hair spilled out of the other. Jeb flew out of the house, the last sound he heard was the tea-kettle hitting the linoleum after he knocked it over.

"Miller County Sheriff's Department, how can I direct your call?"

"I gotta talk to Sheriff Brown. It's urgent."

"I'm sorry," the dispatcher said. "He's not in right now. May I ask who's calling?"

"Is this Sue? It's Jeb McCrary. Look, is he at home? I got his home number."

"Let me check, Jeb..."

"Wait, Sue...I just realized I got his cell. I gotta tell you something else. My arm is white hot today, like it was the day of the tornado. I don't know when or where, but get people safe."

"Okay, Jeb. Thanks."

Jeb hung up with her and called Sheriff Brown's cell.

"Hello?"

"Dale, it's Jeb."

"Jeb, what's wrong?"

"I'm coming up Willow Street," he said. "Mary Lou got out, I know it. Emmy's gone. Theresa's dead, and there was jazz playing in her house. That's Mary Lou's favorite music."

"Jeb, calm down. Theresa's dead?"

"Theresa's dead, yeah. And I know Mary Lou did it. She's headed to the cabin with Emmy, I know she is."

"I've been outside all day. I haven't seen her."

"There's a dirt road behind the barn, Dale." Jeb said. "You wouldn't see it from your land."

"Okay." Sheriff Brown said. "I gotta call this in. If you come up here, you go straight to my house, understand me?"

"Yeah, Dale. Just hurry."

Maybe it was dirt kicking up in the highway behind him, or maybe smoke from burning rubber, but he never made it to his house faster than that. The lights were on. Somebody was in there. He looked in his rearview and saw two sheriff's cars, without lights. He drove past to Sheriff Brown's. The Sheriff was out front, ducked behind a bush with a pair of binoculars.

Jeb hopped out of his truck and closed the door easy. If she was in there, she knew what his truck door sounded like. Of course, she knew how it looked too, but thoughts don't always get through in times like that. The wind, howling all day, was starting to gust. The extra daylight of the summer was being eaten by dark jade clouds.

"Dale, you gotta let me go in." Jeb said.

"No way." Sheriff Brown said. "You could set her off. We're waiting for a SWAT team."

"How far away is one of those?"

"Tulsa."

Jeb shrieked, his knees buckled under him as every stitched nerve in his wrist tore loose. His arm convulsed.

"Jeb, what's happening?"

"Just get me in there, goddammit. I gotta fix this. It's my house."

Dale got Jeb up on his feet. "You got guns in that house?"

"I got a twenty-gauge." Jeb said. "It's got rock salt in it, though."

"She know where it is?"

"No. I hid it, from Emmy, but it's hid."

"I shouldn't do this." The Sheriff said.

"You just get your boys in the basement." Jeb said.

Dale slid a revolver in the back of Jeb's pants.

"I didn't give you that." He said. Hay and small slivers of wood were starting to go airborne.

"Get 'em inside." Jeb said. He walked around Sheriff Brown's gate and stepped onto his property. Debris washed the sky in front of him. He staggered onto the porch, the familiar creak of the rocking chair at full volume until it toppled over. The screen door banged against the door frame.

Jeb grabbed the door and it slammed open. Smooth jazz was playing on the stereo. Emmy was on the couch, still.

Please God, don't let her be-, then he saw her turn over.

"Tranquilizer," came a voice from the kitchen. "I would never hurt our darling."

"What do you want, Mary Lou?"

"I want what's mine." She walked out with a long knife he used for cutting turkey and whole hams. "You left me with nothing, not even a place to live." She tip-toed toward him, pointed in three-sixty. "I want this."

"I want Emmy." Jeb said.

"See? Now we're negotiating. Shouldn't we have done this a long time ago?"

"I suppose so." Jeb sunk, aiming to fall against the cabinets he had built below the front window. He hit it hard enough to smash the lock on it. He could hear a train outside. His arm was radiating torment.

"Oh, did it not heal right?" Mary Lou said. She came closer and closer. Emmy stirred. A gust rocked the house, and Mary Lou hit the floor. Jeb knew he only had one shot.

He popped the remains of the lock off the cabinet as he started to get up. The twenty-gauge was lying on a pile of flannel sheets. He picked it up with his good hand and air cocked it. Mary Lou was on her feet, wiping blood from a cut just above her eye. The house shook again. Jeb aimed and fired.

Mary Lou hit the back wall above Emmy, collapsing on top of her. Even with rock salt, she'd be knocked out from how close she got it. Jeb ran to pick up Emmy, and pulled a flannel sheet from the cabinet to wrap her up in. Then he ran from the house, darting straight for the Sheriff's house.

The roof was starting to come off his cabin as he looked back. The ferocious black center of rotation was turning his barn into confetti strips. He ran, feeling the sting of debris, praying to every God he could find in myth and legend and Sunday Church that some section of pipe or piece of the barn's shrapnel wouldn't impale him or Emmy.

He got to Sheriff Brown's house and turned the corner, hanging low by the cement foundation wall. He coughed and hacked, and pounded on the iron basement door. He slammed with all his might on it, but they couldn't hear. Finally, he pulled out the revolver and shot at the locking mechanism. Sheriff Brown opened the door up, and Jeb handed Emmy in. He had just enough time to get below stairs himself before an aluminum sign flew by, taking the doors with it.

Jeb found his rocking chair, sturdy and intact. He sat on it as he and Sheriff Brown saw all that had come to pass. The Sheriff's house stood. Jed and Emmy would have to stay with him a while as they cleaned up.

Emmy tugged at Jeb's arm, which was free of pain.

"What happened to our house, daddy?"

Jed looked at the pile of rubble that had once played smooth jazz and entertained thoughts of Paris and Egypt.

"Mommy took it, honey." He said. "Mommy took it all away."

The Prophet

"The truth will set you free."

The Prophet's voice boomed. That's what he called himself; *the prophet.* He stood six foot tall. Bigger than life, it seemed to the three hostages cuffed to a steel railing in the abandoned meat-packing plant. Or maybe it was the .357 Magnum, its chrome shining in the fluorescent lights overhead.

He wore a dark brown bomber jacket, olive slacks and dress shoes. He looked through aviator shades, and he had a thin mustache, his hair neatly combed, parted on the right. Springs of hair shot up from the part-line.

Each hostage was picked as a "contestant," offered ten-thousand dollars, to be picked up at that 'haunted' warehouse. All they had to do was handcuff themselves to the railing of the old rusted-out meat-locker, and whoever could hold out the longest without asking to be un-cuffed won it. The Prophet had the fliers made and sent, the website looking sharp on a basic inspection, and a P.O. Box office for return-reply email. He greeted them as they came in with a key in his one hand and the cash in a briefcase in his other hand, presumably holding ten large. There were soft-glow lights and professional video cameras opposite the wall, though there was nobody manning the production equipment.

He set down the briefcase, and pulled out a large picture. He walked around the room, showing the picture to everyone chained up.

"This is my son, Colby," he said. "He was murdered six months ago." He pointed the gun around the room.

"Each of you know the truth, or part of the truth, behind his murder." He said. "Now, I ask each of you... Do you want the truth, or the lie?"

He walked over to Suzy. She was a waitress in the diner his son hung out in. She hung with a bad crowd, one that was sinking their talons into his boy.

"The truth, or the lie?" He asked as he pressed the barrel into the square of her forehead.

"You're fucking crazy." She cried.

He laughed. "You came to an abandoned warehouse and chained yourself to a rail because some spam mail told you that you could win ten thousand dollars. And I'm crazy?" He said with unnerving calm. "Now, I'll say it again. Do you want the truth, or the lie?"

"The truth." She said.

"You lured Colby to a party to make your gangster boyfriend jealous," he said. "You didn't care what happened to him - in fact, you wanted your boyfriend to hurt him to show he still cared about you." He pulled the trigger. Blood sprayed on the wall, the floor and on two of the others. Shouts and screams echoed to no one that cared to hear them.

The Prophet walked over to the next guy. He turned his head away, and the prophet pinned the side of his head to the wall with the barrel.

"The truth or the lie?" He said.

"Does it matter?" The guy said. Silence. Then the Prophet spoke.

"You were her boyfriend's best friend, Eric," He said. "You lured my son outside after getting him very drunk. You watched the alley while he was getting choked and beaten to death." He blew Eric's mind…onto the last hostage.

Colby's killer.

He backed up. "Do you want the truth or the lie?"

"You know the truth, just give me the lie," he said, his lip quivering.

"I'll give you both," The Prophet said as he released the handcuffs from the corpses. "You beat and choked my son to death in that alley." He took the cuffs and made sure both of his last hostage's hands were secured to the rail.

"One more truth," He said as he moved to grab for his briefcase. "You won't be able to muscle that railing off with your bodyweight."

The Prophet adjusted his shades, and headed for the inner door of the room, once the meat freezer locker.

"Wait." The last hostage said. "What about the lie? I asked for the lie."

The Prophet turned his head as he went to grab for the rusty door handle.

"Oh, that," he said. "Someone will hear you scream within a couple of days."

The Prophet closed the solid iron door to the first salvo of a killer's screams.

Uno

They played in the break room of a defunct warehouse a few blocks from the port. Ramsey tossed the wildcard onto the pile. "Draw four. Red. Ha!" He nodded to Dick.

"Fuck!" Dick drew. No reds; his brow furrowed.

"Can you believe this shit?" He said. "We're in the middle of this mess, and he's got us playin' fuckin' *Uno*."

"He's the boss," Sam said through his shit-eating grin, "He says *play games* and we play."

"Yeah, well this whole place is a big, ugly mess." Dick glared about, shuffling the cards in his hands.

The ghostly accouterments of wage slavery decorated the walls around them; a time card punch on the far wall read a frozen 4:50, time cards and schedule sheets bore the yellow stains of age, a calendar was framed in obscene scrawlings etched into the exposed sheet-rock.

Ramsey's eyes darted to the woman. He rolled them up as he picked up a card. "She's wreckin' my concentration," he said, "Why don't we kill that bitch now?"

"Oh shut the fuck up!" Dick said, "Ya' act like you're playin' a fuckin' *chess game*, for cryin' out loud!"

All four glanced over at the source of Ramsey's ire. Four hostages lined the far wall. Grain sacks covered their heads, with holes poked around their noses. Beneath the colored sacks, their mouths were secured with duct tape. Their wrists and ankles were bound behind them. The woman was writhing about, whimpering through the tape.

"No one gets killed 'til we finish the game." Sam said. "That's the rules." He changed it to blue with a seven.

"I hate rules." Ramsey puffed on a Fuente Fuente Opus X, one he'd saved for the completion of the heist. None of them had anticipated this complication, but Ramsey wasn't about to let it get in the way of a victory smoke.

"Goddammit, will you put that fuckin' thing out?" Dick said. "Yer' stinkin' up the whole damn place with that log."

Ramsey chuckled. "Are you serious?" He waved it about in a billiards grip. "We're in a warehouse, Dick. Would you rather smell diesel fuel mixed with sweaty balls? 'Cause that's what I smelled when I got here."

"That thing smells like cat piss."

"That's the smell of luxury, my friend..."

"..or dirty ghetto."

"Guys, guys..." said Sam. "Enough. Let's just get this game over with." He glanced over at Ramsey "Let me get a pull of that thing..."

"Oh no, my man," Ramsey smiled as he leaned back. "Few things are more sacred than a man's cigar." He reached into his jacket, pulling out a pocket humidor. He thumbed it open, and held it out for Sam to grab one.

"Oh God, not you now, Sam..."

"C'mon, Dick. Be a man."

"I am a man," Dick said, "and I'd like to be an *old man* someday..."

"You are in the wrong line of work for that, my friend!" Aaron said. They all laughed.

"YES! Thank you!" Aaron stood up to slap down a blue reverse. Sam threw a Draw Two, and smirked at Ramsey as he skipped him.

"Gimmee that cigar back."

Sam blew out a cloud. "Few things are more sacred than a man's cigar..."

Dick threw a blue seven, leaving him with two cards.

"Uh-oh," Aaron said as he threw a skip on Sam, "Up to you, Ramsey," He raised his hand up an inch, tipping them towards Dick. "We both got two."

"When'd you nail one last?" Ramsey asked Dick.

"This morning."

"Aaron?"

"Yesterday."

Ramsey deliberated before he threw his wildcard. *Draw Four.* "Let's see what ya' got, Aaron." Dick gave the obligatory *fuck you*, picked up four cards and Ramsey called it, "Green."

Aaron threw down his own wildcard. "Guess it doesn't really matter what color, right?"

"Nah, Aaron; just call it." Sam said.

"Uno"

"I hope it ain't a wildcard," Ramsey said.

Aaron, glanced at his remaining card, his face hard as the I-beams holding the place up. "Nope." He flipped it. Blue seven.

"Damn quietest one of the bunch, too..." Ramsey muttered.

Aaron grabbed the .38 Special laying on the table next to the discard pile. He got up slowly. He let out a yawn as he walked towards the wall.

Each sack cloth was a different color. He stopped at blue, aiming the .38 point blank.

"Sorry, pal," he cocked the hammer. "Nothin' personal."

Just a Guy

People get the wrong idea about people like me; the muscle, that is. They think you owe money to a loan-shark, we break your legs with a baseball-bat, crush your hands in vice grips. That looks good in movies, sure. But it's bad business.

First of all, you owe my boss money. I break your legs, your arms, you can't work. I hurt your family, you go to the Feds, brings heat on me and my boss. We don't need that. We just want to get paid.

Some guys go to us all the time, the real degenerates, and they know to have the cash, plus the vig, in my hands when I come to the door. Does that mean I trust them? No. But I might give them an extra day or so; of course, with interest accrued on the vig. That's my take home. My boss wants one vig, usually ten percent; maybe my vig is twenty percent, and I keep the change. My boss could give a rat's ass. That's how it works.

So I come to your house and you don't pay. I might just stop by your job or wait till your wife is home alone and have a talk with her about how you are spending away the money *she's* been saving. Maybe you tell me you're done paying. That might work. Or maybe I'll kick you so hard in your gut I'll need to clean puke of my shoes later. Or maybe even better; I take a pair of jumper cables and clamp 'em to your ears, pull a little. Sure it'll leave a mark, but you can still work.

And oh, if you want to avoid me? Hope I get tired of trying? If my boss agreed to lend you money, I already know your home address, telephone number, cell number, where you work, where you hang out, who you hang out with, where your girl, your wife, your kids work or go to school, and probably what hooker's your favorite. I don't have to threaten people. I just have to show up at all the places you don't think I know about. Because someone has to pay my boss, and your gambling addiction sure as hell ain't comin' out of my pocket.

My boss calls me, and maybe he's got eight other guys besides me that he calls. But he's got a boss that calls him, and that guy's got eight other guys, who have eight guys of their own. I don't know the "big boss" who sits in dark, smoky rooms with his underbosses; wouldn't know him if he walked right past me on the street; even if I did know who he is, not a nod or a wink or a word be said. All I know is my boss. It's all insulated like that. Think of it as a pyramid; think of it as the Amway of crime. I'm just a guy who collects from gamblers and people desperate for a loan, no matter the cost.

Need some money?

The Last Hit

The baked, cracked mud caked the road like dandruff as they drove the Monte Carlo, engrossed in Jimi Hendrix wailing on *Hey Joe* from a beat-up cassette in the tape-deck. The sun was a shimmering blur edging on the rear-view, just starting its descent toward the rock outcroppings that lined the horizon. John was driving, window rolled down half-way to catch the hot breeze. Ellis was riding shotgun, rolling a tooth-pick around in his parched lips as he stared aimlessly out the window. The road they were on didn't have a name, wasn't on a map, and the place they came from wouldn't exist until some idiot real-estate developer decided to put a yuppie oasis over the bones it held.

John and Ellis were swapping shifts driving. They had to make it from the middle of the Mohave to New Orleans in a day. Not impossible, but they had to go low profile. With enough heat in the trunk to take out a small street gang, they couldn't afford a traffic stop.

"We only needed the forty-five," Ellis said as he pulled the tooth-pick out of his mouth. "We didn't have to bring your whole arsenal.."

"All I could find was Bennie to hold the fort back home." John replied. "He knows I'll nap him if he robs me when I'm

in the city, but...I don't know...Don't trust him with my
collection when we're this far out, ya' know?"

"Since when did you have the shakes about Bennie?"

John sighed. "Forever, I guess? I don't know; I took him
on cause of the old man..." John said. "He was a kid back
then; got jumped by the local street-scum. Hell, I felt bad for
him. Tried to get him into the trade, but..." He hesitated.

"But what?" asked Ellis. "He shoot himself in the foot?"

"Nah, nothing like that... I caught him aiming his
twenty-two in the mirror.. sideways."

Ellis laughed. "Sideways? You kiddin' me?"

"Nope'..."

"Kids..." They drove off the dirt road onto a highway
that fed into I-40 East. In a couple of hours, they'd be out of
the desert. The setting sun turned the horizon into a desert
postcard in oil paint. The red unnerved John a little. This last
hit felt wrong, even though everything was above-board, as
much as it got in his world.

"Bennie's balls weren't in his sack."

"Never heard that one before..." Ellis chuckled.

"I don't work with people who don't have the balls, the brains and the heart...Bennie ain't got any of that...why I don't trust him much."

They were quiet for a while as they drove, occasionally commenting on road-kill as they passed some, idle shit-talk. They had long since hit 287 South, which would take them through Dallas-Forth Worth. With over a thousand miles to drive, the night drove them half the way, cups of day-old gas-station sludge and beef-jerky drove them the other half.

Ellis nudged John when they were passing through Fort Worth.

"Didn't that one feel weird to you?" He asked.

"A little." John said. "I mean, a hit's a hit. It was a *custom hit,* but still a hit. Old man gave the order *himself...*"

"Why out there? Like that?"

"Guy used to work Vegas back in the fifties, Ellis," John said, "That's how they did things back then."

"Strange...think he felt guilty?"

John shrugged. "Who knows?"

"You ever feel guilty, John?" Ellis asked.

"Every day..." John replied. The windshield sparkled with the lights of Dallas on the interstate.

"Why do it, then?"

John lit up a cigarette, his first in the whole trip. "I don't miss. And I don't leave collateral damage. I don't hit targets with wives and kids...I do my homework; I make sure they got it comin'...I turn down more hits than I take."

"So you're what, *righteous?*" Ellis stifled a laugh.

"Oh, I'm goin' to hell, no doubt there," John replied. "But think about it...We're killers. The evil, the intent, the true *murderers* are the ones who pay us. Ya' wanna' know how I got started in the trade?"

"Do tell." Ellis said, trading his pulpy toothpick for a cigarette.

"You know I was born in New Orleans. I lived in a bad neighborhood in New Orleans East." He paused, cleared his throat. "A man in the neighborhood, Masterson was his last name, I forget his first – he paid a crack-head fifty bucks to kill his wife... She was cheating on him or some shit... Anyways, that's when crack was new, the early '80s." John flicked his ash out the window. "Crack-head got his hands on an Uzi, don't ask me how – and he just sprayed, man. Killed the wife...and my cousin, and sent a bunch of other people to the hospital." John paused again. "She was four. It took her a week to die."

"Sorry to hear that John, but...That's a reason to become a *cop,* not a hit-man."

"Thought about it," John said, "but cops need a warrant to wipe their asses. I get paid to do what cops wish they could do. I never put an innocent man in the dirt...until today."

"Yeah, that's what's bugging me."

"The old man's always given me good targets, never had a complaint against him. But with the brain tumor, the prognosis...He had to put out the hit to protect the ones he loved."

Before they realized it, they were on I-10, a half-hour away from New Orleans. They would crash at John's for a few hours, and go meet the old man's wife to help her plan for the memorial service. Not that it would be in the papers.

"So what do we tell her about the old man?" Ellis asked.

John rolled his window all the way down, flicked out the butt and glanced at the cherry spiraling out like a dull jumping jack.

"He went out on his own terms," John said, "Quick, and painless."

The Ghost

Gunfire, hot lead erupting down the chamber like magma as the gas escapes and the sound of glass shattering, three dead and two holding on to life by their quickly-emptying clips. Sparks snap on metal, dust pops from the brick wall behind the angry ghost. He lights the white lightning-soaked rag and tosses the bottle, savoring the sound of glass breaking, flames soaking and mooks screaming in immolation. A few more shots, then clicks. The ghost reloads with one of nine clips strapped to his body. He doesn't want to shoot the guys that are on fire as he goes for the front door, but he doesn't need witnesses. Needs before wants. Two rounds, dead drops with flames licking at their Italian suits.

The ghost fades into the alleyway, his heartbeat still as the blueprints for Grainger's hideout flashes through his head. He has an unsecured access from the roof. It's a climb, and he'll have to fit a small charge on the power coming in. That's what makes the hideout a fortress; security. Grainger knows he's there, looking at him now through a security camera in the alleyway.

The ghost jumps up on the dumpster and that's the last Grainger will see him before he'll be worm-food. By the time the other mooks hit the alley, the ghost will once again be a ghost.

He blows the power first; just a *pop* as the charge goes off. The roof is huge. It has to be; there's a heliport and a chopper on it. Grainger's escape plan. He'd needs it today as the ghost pulls out his cellphone.

The Grainger hideout has excellent security – he knows. He put it in. He also put in dummy cams filled with C4, lined the wall with small charges behind the sheetrock. Everything is timed by a Trojan horse installed in the security company's web server. He dials in and feel the rumblings shake the building. Was Grainger dead? No. Not the point. The ghost faces a locked door on the roof; the escape hatch.

An explosion rocks his car out front. Again, part of the plan. Grainger won't think it's safe to go out front. He has only two escape options, and the first will now be seen as unsafe. His pilot is on standby at all times. The ghost moves to the side of the door as he hears motion. The door flies open and five goons, the chopper pilot, and Grainger run out. The ghost moves.

Gunfire. Head-shots, the roof now littered in corpses. Only two remain; the pilot and Grainger.

"Who the fuck are you?" Grainger reaches for his back. The ghost shoots him in the shoulder, just enough to shred the muscle.

"Argh!" Grainger falls like a pussy. The ghost has one eye trained on him, one on the pilot.

"Take out your guns, both of you, and kick 'em over."

"Whattaya' want, money?" Grainger says. "We can work something out."

"You're running little girls for pedophiles," the ghost says. "I want them all."

"You got it," Grainger said. "I'll just make a call. Where do you want them?"

"Make your call." The ghost keeps his eyes trained as Grange pulls out his cell and dials a number.

"Shit. I got no signal," he says.

"I know. Your cell's been inactive for twenty-four hours. I didn't want to alert you before I had a chance to kill all your cohorts. You're the last one."

"Bullshit! I got a hundred guys."

"No. You *had* about twenty guys who knew how to wipe their noses. The rest weren't loyal enough to you to take a bullet for ya'. Sorry."

"You still want the girls-,"

"Shut the fuck-up, scumbag. I *have* the girls, the cars, the guns, the dope... Your whole empire. Well, the police have most of that stuff. Except for one girl they'll never find out about."

"Who?"

"My daughter," the ghost says. "One of your thugs kidnapped her six months ago. That's why I'm here."

"Look, I'm sorry. It was just business."

The ghost shoots him in the other shoulder. Grange screams out in pain.

"I know all about business. I used to work for the government, did you know that?" He says. "Never mind.. Stupid question. I was trained Special Forces, ran black ops for the CIA...Every hell-hole or crater in the world has my footprints or blood drops in the soil. I've done many terrible things in the name of *business.*"

The ghost chuckles. "Once, I put exactly one thousand sewing needles into a guy, *one thousand,* and hooked them up to wires." He looks at Grainger's face, which is getting ashen white. "And that was just to wake him up."

"So you gonna' torture me?"

"No. I'm dead actually, a star in the lobby at Langely. I'm a ghost, as far as the world is concerned. I don't even have fingerprints anymore. So I'm not *in the business* of torturing people."

"So what? You're just gonna kill me?"

"Nope." The ghost says as the pilot draws a forty-five from his back, slides the barrel down and plasters the concrete with skull chips and chunks of Grainger's hard-wiring.

"The thousand needles story? Really, Jimmy?"

"I did do that once, Joe."

"I'll believe it when I see it."

"Pass out at my house again," Jimmy smiles, "I'll show you." He winks.

"No, I'll take your word." Joe says. "So where to?"

"How about Paraguay?" Jimmy says. "I got a set-up there."

"We can make money, I guess."

"A fortune."

Jimmy and Joe hop into the chopper. Joe runs through the checklist, and soon they're off the landing pad, heading for the Miami skyline.

Joe looks back to the roof.

"One thing I can say about the prick," Joe says, "He paid well."

They both laugh.

King of the World

Cole sat impatiently in the office of the old warehouse on Wharf Road. That was the meeting point. He knew the rest of the crew would show; he had the money, over a million tucked in a canvas mail bag. Jack, Mickey and George would be there any minute. They just had to tie up loose ends.

Jack popped through the door, out of breath. He grabbed a chair and sat down, reaching into his overcoat to pull out a flask. He took a swig and looked at Cole, his arm propped on the table.

"Where're Mickey and George."

"Full a' lead." Jack said as he caught his breath. "Cops aired 'em out."

"They onto us?"

"Nah, I ditched 'em good."

Cole held up the bag. "Going by weight, we got more than a million in here."

"We're rich men, Cole."

Cole nodded. "We gotta' lay low for a while-"

"We're buyin' a luxury boat."

"Did you hear what I just said?"

"I got a guy; he's gotta' trash a brand new one for scrap 'cause he ain't got room on his land." Jack said, "He says he'll give it to me *off-the-books* for fifty large."

"So what, you want to take a cruise?"

"I wanna' lay low, like you said. We grab our dames and go down to the Caribbean for a few months."

"Jane will never go for it," said Cole, "She didn't like this idea to begin with."

Jack slapped Cole's arm. "Tell her it's only for a week. The heist won't be in the papers til' tomorrow. We can leave tonight - just tell her we never went through with it."

Cole thought about it. Jane did need some relaxing.

"Okay," he said, "but she's gonna' find out eventually."

"Yeah," Jack said, "*Eventually.* Let's worry about right now."

They sailed for the Bahamas that night. Everything was easy. Cole felt like the king of the world, and Jane seemed to be enjoying herself. Jack and Marion lay on the deck, peering up at the stars. Cole stood against the rail, peering out at the expanse of ocean as it met the stars. God, they were so big, so many out there. Jane bounced up next to him in nothing but her swimsuit.

"Let's swim, Cole." She said.

"I don't know...we're awfully far out here...plus we can't see..."

"That's okay, buddy," Jack said, "I'll leave the light on. You'll be able to find the boat."

Cole was hesitant. But the look on Jane's face; he hadn't seen it in years. Carefree, every bit the flapper he hooked himself to in the first place. And he was king of the world. Why couldn't he swim in his ocean?

Jane jumped in, and that settled it. He stripped to his boxers and jumped in after her. The water was warm, and he could hear the splashes coming from Jane's swimming. She had a lead on him, but he caught up to her eventually. They held each other, playfully kissing. They could barely see the light from the boat. He was thinking they should get back when the light went out. He heard the roar of the motor over the waves. He and Jane shouted, but no one could hear them. Eventually the sound of the motor couldn't be heard over the waves.

"Was that your plan, Jack?"

Jack looked over at Marion. "They were both swimmers in high school. I knew they wouldn't be able to pass up a swim in the ocean."

"How'd you know they'd both go together?"

Jack took Marion in his arms.

"Cause I'm the king of the world, doll," he said with a smile, "and you're my queen."

Lakeview

The street was piled to either curb with mud and debris, like the dirty snowbanks I'd known and loved back home. But there was no snow there, just mud. New Orleans didn't get snow that could pile up like that. We were driving in Lakeview, an upper-class neighborhood bordering Lake Ponchartrain. I was jonesin' for a smoke, but we were in a car belonging to Catholic Community Services of Baton Rouge. The most I could get was a window cracked, and the smell quickly convinced me to close the crack for the sake of Jeannette, Jake, Don and Kyla, our guide from CCSBR.

We saw people parked off to the side, pristine cars in the aftermath of a meteorological apocalypse. They weren't trapped in Lakeview; those cars belonged to people who evacuated New Orleans before Katrina hit. We drove by a older black gentleman, sitting in a chair in front of an open garage. I thought I saw a shot-gun. Just a guy protecting his home, or someone paid to protect another's home. He just sat there, his eyes not leaving us until we turned the corner.

"We're coming up at the site of the Seventeenth Street Canal breech," Kyla said as she slowed down, looking for a place to pull over. We wanted to see it first hand; hell, we *needed* to see it first-hand.

We were headquartered in Baton Rouge, the capital of Louisiana, and the biggest city near New Orleans. It was about a hundred miles north of the Crescent city, and while we were driving through the physical devastation, the *human* devastation was staying in every motel, hotel, shelter and relative's house in Baton Rouge. We were fresh from Albany, about to spend three weeks providing assistance to evacuees every day, doing paperwork, hearing stories told by people who were too raw emotionally to put up the iron wall that would be cast in a couple months. We needed to be where they'd been; try to understand what hell they'd been trapped in for four- or five days. We had to see it.

Kyla pulled over on a block flanked by a concrete wall. She, and we, got out. I turned my camcorder on as we stretched our legs.

She pointed to a house that had a roof sloped into a sharp point.

"This house right here is the direct path," she said. "The roof is slanted because the water just clobbered it. The chunks of canal blew out the back of the house."

"Can we go back there?" Jake asked.

"I wouldn't," Kyla said. "Everything here is dangerous. And remember as you walk around to wear your masks."

I needed a smoke. As I walked away, pulling my mask off on the sly, I commented, under my breath, that I was a smoker, and I'd be dead quicker anyway. I wish the microphone didn't pick it up, but.... oops.

I saw many things; the neon 'X' search markers that had the date in the top corner, the search party abbreviations in the right, something I didn't know in the left, and the dreaded bottom sector - the number found inside. I saw the waterlines on the houses, the dirt and grime, the mold - but two things that day underscored the rest of what I would learn down there.

One was a porcelain statue of a tiny cherub placed intentionally on a tree stump. That was one. Someone's child was lost, and it was a memorial, like the crosses that dotted highways.

The second thing, propped up by a mish-mash of particle-board home furnishing, weathered and moldy, was an American flag, flapping in the winter breeze coming off of the lake. It was worn and dirt beat. It was a desperate symbol of patriotism, or cynicism.

In the days to follow, I would debate over and over which symbol it was.

God's Country

A lonely street sign stood crooked against the wind in front of Saint Mary's Church, *Open for prayer*, it said. A couple of old birds got out of a grey Ford Focus, ambled out on to the sidewalk, strolled in to encase their petitions to the Almighty in brick and stained glass and the scented votive candles in sanguine red glass holders.

I don't pray in churches. I only need to pray behind shellacked-pine bars in the middle of fucking nowhere when the bottles above are giving up their spirits to automatic lead, drowning me in frontier holy water.

There's no atheists in foxholes or country-bar shootouts. I'm looking at Ned, and he's looking up at the Genesee neon sign above, and he's saying prayers, making the barest trace of a cross on his chest. Fifteen minutes ago, he didn't believe in nothing except the kilo of uncut blow in his belly, strung like cellophane sausage-links.

At the bar a week ago, sitting at a table that had a few less holes in it, I told him what I thought of his "faith."

"Man, that's fuckin' stupid." We were sitting side-by-side at a half-table bolted to the wall, staring out the front window, watching the dusty Texas dandruff set aloft by a passing F-150. Just me, Ned, and Clem, the bartender. If not for the weekend line dances, the place would've been tumbleweed years ago.

"C'mon, Blake, easy money, man." Ned popped a Mentos.

"You don't know these people."

"I know Shawn. He knows 'em."

"Shawn doesn't know a condom." I looked around, "Fuck, half this town is his bastard kids."

"Shawn's alright," Ned said.

"Look, I like Shawn, but he's in over his head this time, kid."

"What's the big deal? I go over the border, they fill me up with baggies, I come back and shit 'em out. No big deal."

"Assuming you don't get caught by border patrol, *big* assumption, what if one of them breaks inside ya?"

"It'll be fine."

"Yeah, you'll just smile, give a *thumbs up* like in those damn Mentos commercials and just like that, everything's just gonna be A-Okay, right?"

"You should talk, Blake," Ned said. "You're no angel."

"I've been 'no angel' successfully for thirty years, and not by doing dumb shit like this."

"I'm gonna' do it, Blake. Sarah needs it for the divorce."

"If I were you, I'd pray to God you'll be around to hear me say I told you so."

"I don't believe in God," Ned said. "Just sweet tail. I'm surprised you believe in God."

I took a quencher from my beer bottle. "When I have to."

***

So now I have to. Ned comes back a' cryin'—he can't shit. And Sarah disappeared with his money. I wish I could say I was surprised, that I haven't become some world-worn, cynical old dick, unable to be surprised by anything other than gunfire. But being honest, even gunfire's not a surprise. Ned's gut is pregnant with a kilo of uncut cocaine, and the guys outside are prepping for an emergency C-section. I don't know who's the bigger fool; Ned for doing it, or me for coming to his side when it went south. They say God suffers fools. Hope so.

I'm looking around, I'm out of bullets, and the shotgun Clem kept behind the bar is on the floor in front of the bar in Clem's dead hands. Actually, it probably flew somewhere when they pumped him. But other than that, the inventory I'm taking is bleak. Just beers, glasses, sodas. I'm gazing at two-liter bottles of diet Coke, thinking *who drinks that shit here?* But I must have something else on my mind, as bullets are still tap-dancing along the brass rail. Then the image comes into my eye, and the synapses fire, bringing all the clips and images and words into a coherent story. A half-assed epiphany. Maybe a miracle. Maybe.

"Ned, you still got Mentos?"

"What the fuck kind of question is that?" More than fear, actually.

I grab his collar. "Answer the fucking question!"

"Yeah, I got two packs."

"Okay, just follow my lead."

I grab a white apron and put it on top of a broom handle and raise it. A bullet whizzes by it, then silence.

"You givin' up?" Mexican accent. Not a local.

"Yeah," I say. "Don't shoot! I'm coming up."

I slowly rise, arms to the sky. No one shoots. That's as good as an ice-breaker in situations like this.

"Look," I say. "We have a problem."

"No," a fat fuck in a knock-off Stetson says. " *You* have a problem."

True, but nonetheless.

"Then we both have a problem. They did it wrong."

The Mexicans sweep open the bullet-ravaged door and step in. All casual, 'cause they know we're out in God's country—only God payin' taxes out here. We're both rat-meat if I can't play the game I end when so many others play it with me—the 'Spare my life, please!' game.

I motion the fat one over to the bar. "Get up, Ned," I say, but Ned just groans.

"What they did was, they tied the baggies in one long string," I tell the Mexicans, who by now are guns down. "Makes it easy to pull up, that is, if something doesn't push a baggie into the bowel. That's why you're supposed to do 'em one at a time."

A short, ratty, pock-marked kid with The Virgin Mary scrawled on his bicep comes up with a fucking Bowie knife. "We're getting' our shit, man!"

"Look, you're gonna' get your shit all over this floor if ya cut him up," I say. "Unless you're a doctor with a team, it's impossible to disembowel somebody neatly."

"How you know that?" The kid says.

I get Ned up, arm over my shoulder. "I was dumb enough to wear a thousand-dollar suit once," I say. "Had to burn it, and shower for three hours."

"You sayin' you're a killer, big man?" The fat one says.

"I'm saying I know you can't just cut it out of him and expect product. But I think I can at least salvage some, no cutting needed."

I search Ned's pockets and feel two rolls and pull em out. One is unopened, the other has a few left. I have no clue about any formula or recipe, but I figure you needed the soda in first, 'cause in the video they dropped the Mentos in the Diet Coke, not the other way around. Then I remember the video of the guy I saw. He drank the soda first. I grab a two-liter from the ground, but easy. These guys are still a bit itchy.

"Any of you guys seen the Diet Coke and Mentos trick?"

They're deadpan. The tattoo boy grabs a roll and looks at it like he never saw candy.

I hold up the Mentos. "A couple of these, Drop 'em in enough of this," I hold up the Diet Coke, "causes a chemical reaction. Turns the soda bottle into a volcano of soda."

I look back, know I got enough bottles. I sit Ned on the barstool and open the Diet Coke. I drop two

Mentos in and the Mexicans are, for a moment, wide-eyed at the eruption. Then it ends and we're out of science class.

The third man, a short, lean, muscular hombre dressed in a three-piece Brooks Brothers suit and a black felt fedora, speaks for the first time.

"How does this," he points, "chemical reaction pertain to our friend here?"

This guy seems interested. That's good for me.

"I make him drink the two liter, or as much as he can hold without throwing it up, and they're his Mentos—he likes the shit—and we wait a minute or two for the eruption."

"So he vomits?"

"He'll be blowing it outta' both ends."

The man strokes his chin, forearm resting on a chair back.

"Can your friend handle it? He looks ill."

"It's the blockage. This might be the only thing that'll help him."

I grab one of the other two-liters of Diet Coke and sit Ned up. He looks weary, defeated. Pretty much like he should look. He's clutching his side.

"Ned, I know you're not thirsty, but you're going to drink this whole thing."

Ned looks up at me, eyes puffy. "What if I can't? They'll kill me."

"No, they won't. But I will, you have my word." I shove the bottle in his mouth. "Now drink."

Ned struggles, but I get him to drink almost three-quarters of the bottle. He tries to puke it up a few times. I handle it. I've had to poison people before. It doesn't work if you let 'em puke it up.

"I'm not guaranteeing you'll get all of your product in one piece," I warned them, "But the alternative would get you far less."

I give Ned two Mentos. "Chew them up in your mouth, Ned. Then one gulp, swallow it all."

I back up. "Y'all may want to back up." Ned's face goes bleach white and he contorts in a God-awful way. The Mexicans back up, their eyes wide like Ned is about to go thermonuclear. In a way, he is.

***

A blast of foam shoots out of his mouth like super-rabies and the back of his pants bulge out and turn dark. He collapses on the floor, gagging and convulsing. I know two things are happening: He's choking on baggies, and one of them broke inside. Ned is dead, just waiting for the clock's hand to strike the second. I hop down and pry his mouth open and stick my fingers in as far as I can until I feel slimy plastic. I pull at it slowly, break Ned's jaw open with a wrench on the floor. Like I said, he's dead anyway. The coke is gonna' kill him. Treating him like he's salvageable is gonna kill *me.*

I start pulling up the string of baggies. After the first one, the rest come easy. Shit, there's a ton of 'em. Hopefully a kilo.

"How much was in him, a kilo?" I ask over the bar as the Mexicans look on.

"Why you need to know?" The kid says.

I had a pile of baggies in my hand. "So I know how much is still in him."

"One kilo, yes." The professional says. I pull the last baggie I can out—the one that burst. I tip my hand up and lower it quick, letting the full weight of the baggies hit my palm.

"There's probably still a quarter in him. Let me turn him over." I undo Ned's buttons and yank his corduroys down. Then I spin him, pull down his shitty boxers and pretend the stench doesn't make me want to have an eruption of my own. I grab the surrender apron and give Ned an ass-wipe. A string knot is embedded in his corn-hole and I pull it. All told, four more baggies from the back-door. I take them over to the sink and set all of them in a pan of water. I think twice and squirt some dish-soap in there.

Then I grab a cigarette from my pocket, light it with a wooden matchstick from the bar, my own votive candle. Can't figure if it's for my immortal soul or my very mortal skin.

"Do you know who I am?" The professional says.

"A reasonable man, I hope."

He dusts off a seat before he sits down.

"I don't take a piss for one kilo, Mr. Blake."

Mr. Blake? What?

"Come, sit," he says. I'm not one to argue. I hop over the bar and don't bother dusting off. There are worse things on my clothes.

"Do you think me a fool, Mr. Blake?"

"I don't know you well enough to think anything."

"Which is good, good. But I'm no fool. I would not send the likes of your friend over the border to do my business, nor the fool who recruited him. This, Shawn, was asked to recruit your friend."

I listen. What the hell else do I have to do?

"And I know how to properly bring things through the border. You were right, you do not tie them together, it's...messy. But I instructed this for that reason."

"So he'd die?"

"So he'd come to you when he couldn't pass them. I needed to see you in action."

"I don't get it."

"You will." The man calls out to the other two. "Empty your clips into the mule." He says. They walk over to the bar. The man eyes me hard, pulls a Beretta out of his coat and hands it to me. "You fire three times. He was your friend." He points to the other two who are aiming down, prepared to air out dead Ned. I get up to shoot a corpse in good faith, but the man tugs at my shirtsleeve. I lean down.

"Only two men will leave this bar tonight." His black eyes burned. "Choose wisely."

I could shoot all three of them. Way I figure I have three bullets, if the man at the table isn't full of shit. One for Ned, one each for his triggers. I look back, and he just sits there, staring out the window, like he knows he's walking out, suit unsoiled. He's got an ace. A man who doesn't piss for a kilo of coke doesn't walk around without aces. So I walk up to the bar and shake the gun like Ned's something more than cooling meat on the barroom floor as the triggers empty full clips. Glancing over at me like I'm a pussy, soon to be vic' two. I fire finally, mush out Ned's eye and I hear the toy-sounding clicks of their empty pieces. I push the wiry one with the jailhouse ink into the fat fuck and give them both their last rites.

I hand the gun back to him.

"You didn't point the gun at me. Curious," the man said. "Why not?"

"It's empty."

"And you know this how? The weight?" The man's eyes lit up, a kid, curious.

"You said you don't piss for a kilo." I tapped the Beretta. "Bet you don't load four bullets for a three-bullet job either."

The man laughed. He took off his fedora and held it in his hands.

"I am Javier." He says. "Do you need to clean anything up before we leave for Juarez?"

"Juarez?"

"I have killers, Mr. Blake." He says. "I have many killers. I need thinkers. I have to say that the soda and candy thing was impressive. I'm sure I can find you excellent accommodations and steady employment."

"I don't really have a choice here, do I?"

"You always have a choice. You can believe that if it helps."

I look around at a bar made into a war zone by three men in two hours, in a land where the Law is no friend and my friends become ghosts and holy-rollers preach Judgment Day to the hung-over bastards whose wives go to churches *Open for prayer,* and I realize that I don't really have a choice, or a prayer.

I clean up the Diet Coke and Mentos and my gun, the only things linking me to the carnage at the bar, and join Javier in his inky black Escalade, and this one weird thought comes to mind:

Use a bar for a church, and God might be hammered when he answers your prayers.

Slick Eddie

A phoenix Tale

"Slick Eddie" Phipps walked into the Phoenix Hotel lounge, all BrylCreem and chicken-shit. His hip bop hid the leg shakes, trembling fingers fluffed the silk shirt butterfly collar, unbuttoned to show his man-patch. He killed half a stick of antiperspirant during dress-up, jaw-line to solar-plexus. Benito Moretti, "Bloody Benny": a nickname well earned, Benny shed blood like oak leaves in October. He had a vicious temper and a long memory, he rattled off the names of those who screwed him at every social moment like a morbid opening prayer. The names always changed: crossing Benny quickly put the offender under their own cross, usually granite.

Eddie whistled to the bartender with his two fingers. Barkeep took his sweet time coming down. *Prick.* When he got there, Eddie said, "Hey yeah, lemme' get a Miller High-Life there, chief."

"I'm sorry, we don't carry that," his smile, subtle: *bullshit he was sorry.*

"What kinda place doesn't carry the *High-Life?*" Eddie held up his palms, shrugged and looked at the surrounding bar-flies. No love from the bar.

"That's alright, chief; I'll just get a Bud," he leaned over the bar, "You carry Bud, right?" The bartender slid a Budweiser in front of him.

"That'll be two-fifty." Eddie thought of telling him to start up a tab, but the schlep was giving him deadpan. Plus, he couldn't jerk around too much: He wasn't there for a liver-pounding.

It was fool-proof. That's what he told Benny two months ago with his palm out for seed money. Truckloads of Salvadorans coming into the South End, grant money flying their way from the Mayor, proclamations of "these hard-working people – I wish I had a *whole city* full of them." Simple racket, textbook protection squeeze. Only they already *had* protection – *Ojos Muertos;* international strong-arm club, left bodies around like jumped checkers.

Eddie conned Joe-Joe Moretti to thug up with him when the first mom-and-pops opened. Joe-Joe had a temper, like his old man. They caught some back-talk at the bodega; tough old bird, crow's feet and beady eyes, shooting rapid-fire Spanish, sparked Joe-Joe. He threw a back-hand to her; she screamed bloody murder, *Ave Maria* or some shit. They walked out to the intersection, to a gang of young OM soldiers: baseball-bats, switches and machetes: little stone killers. Eddie only walked away 'cause that crazy son-of-a-bitch Joe-Joe *didn't.*

Eddie wasn't invited to the funeral. These days they didn't use horse-heads. He knew what it meant. Then he got a phone call from Benny himself: an invite to the Phoenix Lounge for dinner. The last and only time Benny called him personally was when Joe-Joe was hiding out at Eddie's with his Latina girlfriend. Benny was from the old country. Now Joe-Joe was dead on his scheme and all the sudden he had a dinner date.

Benny was sitting in the back row of booths. The lounge had potential: marble checkerboard floor-tiles, mahogany bar with black padded-leather trim, mahogany pool-table at center-stage with chrome trim, lit up by an overhead fluorescent covered in stained glass relief; a phoenix, reminded Eddie of Bavarian beer-art. The upper walls were white, turning to cedar panel below the *loner's bar*, lacquered and bottle-ringed, lining the whole place except for the far wall opposite the bar. That's where the booths were. That's where Benny sat, sucking down pasta.

"H-hello, Mr. Moretti," Benny looked up from his meal.

"What are we, strangers all a' the sudden?" He wiped his lips with the napkin, pointed to the far side of the booth, "Sit down, Eddie. Whattaya' wanna' eat? I got a menu right here," He handed Eddie the plastic-laminate menu. Eddie flipped it open and quickly glanced through it.

"I don't know what I want,"

"Don't be shy; get whatever you want," Benny dug back into his linguini, "you make me nervous, ya' sit here and you don't eat."

Benny signaled a waitress, and Eddie ordered a seafood platter. The waitress refreshed his beer. Eddie shifted in his seat, uneasy.

"What? Come out with it," said Benny, "You wanna' know if there's a beef over Joe-Joe."

"Well, yeah, I mean, Mr., er, *Benny,* you have no idea how sorry-"

Benny laughed, set down his napkin.

"Kiddo, Joe-Joe took after me, skin ta' skin," He said, "He dug his own pit, they just lowered him in. Don't you worry about a thing; Life is for the living, eh?" He let out a full-gut laugh, clamping his massive palm on Eddie's shoulder. Eddie prayed he didn't notice the trembling. He smiled, tested the water, then he joined Benny laughing.

They talked about old times as his plate arrived. All kinds of old memories; even Joe-Joe's Latina girlfriend came up. He sat across from the only man in the world he feared, and he couldn't help but feel like he was dining out with his dad.

"Ass 'ole," Eddie and Benny looked up to see a young man, not old enough to even be *in* there. "You hit my siss 'er..."

"Get outta' here," Benny replied, turning back to his plate, "quit botherin' me,"

"No!" The kid said. Eddie could tell by his voice he was slow.

Benny dropped his napkin. "Kid, if ya' know what's good for ya'..."

"Fuck you, ass 'ole!" The kid spit it out, a mist of dribble landing on both their plates.

Benny got red in the face. The kid wasn't moving. Eddie saw his chance to do Benny a solid. He got up from the booth and clamped his hand down on the kid's shoulder. The kid lunged toward Benny: Eddie pulled him back, heard the sound of silverware crashing to the ground. Then pain; then the rush of blood from his punctured lung stung his lips as it spilled out. The slow kid still had a handle on the knife, and he bent it up. Eddie crashed to the floor in shock, and soon he was enveloped in cold chill, vision fading to the last thing he saw: Benny gently patting the kid's arm.

"Did I do OK, Uncle Benny?"

Benny put his finger to his lips. "Keep your voice down," he whispered, "How long ya' been off the pills?"

The kid held up his fingers. "Three-, no, four days."

"OK, good, now the cops are gonna' take you down to the station. You just call Jeffrey, act as nutty as you can until either he gets there or they drug ya'. Ya' got all that?" The kid nodded.

Benny smiled. "Good." He took the last sip of wine he'd get before the cops got there. "Good boy. You'll grow up to be the son I never had." He got up when the strobe of the cruisers lit the back wall. He stepped over the punctured body of "Slick Eddie."

"Putz."

Do Him

The first time I saw Jessica, she was sitting in the back of McClatchkeys, her raven hair and dark eyes dotting the dimly-lit table in noir. Nick told me she did the dirty stuff. And Congressman Miller had a wandering eye, wandering from his wife and his Miller tribe, anyways. The hypocrite paraded them around on every campaign, holding them up like first-prize hogs, fat off the pork of his office. He needed a scandal. And I needed to have it before the Primary.

Nick made the appointment. I slid down across from Jessica, if that was her real name, and introduced myself. She was reading a newspaper, how, I don't know. She said her name without looking up.

"So, uhh... Nick told me you can... take care of problems...." I said.

"If you had enough money, I could stop climate change, baby," she said with a crimson-lipstick smile. "Did Nick tell you my price?"

"Yeah, twenty, right?"

"Yup," she said, "and I assume that it's in your briefcase. Slide it over."

I slid the briefcase over, twenty thousand dollars in unmarked bills. Twenties, mostly. I could hear her flipping through it, seemed like forever, but she closed it and tucked it between her legs.

"So, can you, umm.... do him?"

"That's what I get paid for," she said.

"Make it dirty," I said, feeling a bit more comfortable. "I want his balls on a silver platter."

"No problem," she said.

The crowd was noisy. I felt more emboldened by the fact that, from where we were, no one could see or hear us.

"Can you get it on video?" She looked up with ice in her eyes.

"No. Absolutely not," she said.

"Well, can you take still shots?" I asked. How was I gonna nail him for doing dirty and nasty on his wife without proof?

"I can take stills. That's not a problem. I have a Polaroid."

I was a little nervous. *Wouldn't he know?* But Nick said she was a pro, and Nick knew his pros.

"When and where do you want to meet back up?" She said.

"I'm staying at the hotel next door. Room 306. I have a spare room card. Just come on in when you're done. I'll be up all night."

Jessica got up with my, now her, briefcase and I sat there for a while. I didn't want to leave with her. When she was clear out of sight, I paid my tab and hopped over to the hotel.

The wait was agonizing. I kept replaying every scenario where this could go wrong. He could sense she was a plant, he wouldn't let her take pictures, hell, he'd already be in the room with another hooker – everything I could imagine pumped through my racing pulse. Sweat cooled me in the hot motel room. I opened the minibar and threw the cap off a cheap bottle of vodka, holding it to my lips for a quick nip.

At one-thirty a.m. the door slid open. It was Jessica. She was wearing different clothes, and her hair was blond. She had a plastic bag double wrapped, reminded me of the times I had to use a plastic bag to pick up my dog's shit when I walked him. She had a manila envelope in her other hand. She tossed both on his bed.

I picked up the manila envelope, and there were Polaroids inside. I picked up the first one, and my eyes grew wide with shock. I leaned over and threw my whole future up on the floor, mixed with vodka.

"Oh my God!" I said.

"I did him," she said. "Have a look in the bag."

I was in tremors when I opened the bag. Inside of it were two bloody testicles, still half wrapped in the Congressman's scrotum.

"What? Why?"

"You wanted them," Jessica said as she turned to leave, "Sorry, I couldn't find any silver platters at this hour."

A Gentleman's Game

Javier DeSantana's dark face was the night sky, his eyes rimmed red with capillaries, perfect teeth in a smile that only monsters smiled. He had on a burgundy cashmere suit with a yellow shirt and a white tie, both silk. It was Brooks Brothers, by the look. I knew Javier had a taste for luxury; probably paid twenty large for it. He was ill-fitted in a fifth-wheel trailer in the middle of the woods of Montgomery County. The Devil himself in God's country among the sticks and the muck and the bullfrogs.

I didn't know the guy sitting next to him. That was well enough; he probably didn't know my guy. Besides, neither of them were on the board.

"This is an..." Javier pressed his finger to his lips, "..*odd* way of sorting out our situation."

"Look at the alternative, Javier."

Javier stared at the board, marble, the wood pieces looked out of place. I bought those to make marking them easier.

"You know how our games turn out, Michael," he said. "How they *always* turn out. Are you sure you want to play this?"

"Yeah. Seems the best way. I'll take my chances."

Javier tipped his fingers to his guy, a meaty man with a bald head to match Javier's. I nodded to my guy. They pulled out notepads and pens.

Javier made the first move, sliding his pawn up two spaces. I mirrored his move.

"Don't they always start like this?" Javier said.

"Our chess games, or turf wars?"

Javier cast his gaze out the window behind me.

"Perhaps both?" His eyes returned to the board. With pursed lips he moved his knight out.

"We were friends once." I said, making my move.

Javier sighed. "I'd like to think we are still that... friends..." He drew first blood, capturing a pawn with his knight. It was the beginning of a scorched-earth exchange, many pieces to be taken in quick exchange. But maybe not so quick; he flipped the pawn over, showing me the name written in blue pen on a round sticker.

Art Dooley

Art Dooley was a local chap, a player, pumped crystal to tweakers on Central Ave. He was a utility player. He'd rough somebody up for an extra couple bucks, but he was replaceable. I nodded with a mock solemnity as Javier showed the piece to his man, who scribbled the name on his notepad.

"You know what you did, Javier," I said as I circled my other knight in my hand, "You upset the order of things."

"I thought they needed to be upset." Javier replied in a calm, flat tone. "I had my reasons."

I guess it was inevitable. Javier dealt in the elected, with pinstripe suits and flag pins who spent lonely weeks in Albany, always in need of that thing "the people" rarely knew about; the coke, the X, the unsophisticated hookers who looked good enough to have their way with, but dumb enough not to watch "Politics Tonight" on the local station. One day, Javier "requested" a single mom; a whore, but a mother. I thought one of the pols just wanted to "save her", or have that knight in shining armor trip. But nope. The sick bastard just wanted the kid.

Now, I'm scum. I don't have the pretense of Javier. I'm a degenerate, pure and simple. But I don't do kids. Crack whores? Sure. But kids? Not a chance.

I find out what went down and I'm furious at Javier but I have to play it cool. Maybe he didn't know. So I do just that. We sit, playing chess, talking about the weather; fuck, I forget what we were really talking about, but I bring it up.

No shock, no anger crossed his face.

"So was he satisfied with the experience?"

If I had known beforehand that Javier would see it like that, I'd have prepped the gang and it would've been a turf war. But as we talked, we knew it was inevitable. We were growing, getting our foothold, and he was becoming a player himself. He could have been a pawn on the board, but I still showed him respect. He still had guns. I had a family. He did too. We both knew the cost of an all-out battle. So, as we began with Javier's jade pieces and pass-time games, now we play with wood and real stakes.

The exchange went down; three pawns, a knight and a bishop. I lost Timmy Harrigan, my guy on the books. Nobody could beat Timmy; he could launder gains chlorine-clean. He was the bishop. Javier's face contorted slightly as his knight was taken. Juan Plantana, a good gun. A real good gun.

I watched Javier plotting his next move. He clasped his slender hands, veins bulging. He was strategizing. He was playing chess in the Mansion on State when I first came to make his acquaintance.

I was leading a new school of sharks from Boston; the heat was on there. We had a stripper wound up drowned in a toilet at *The Sparkle*, a club on Lagrange Street. It couldn't be tied to us, not conclusively, but we had to crouch by the fences in our operations. Can't do business like that.

New York was 'connected' – too much family politics. Organized crime in New York was a fucking bureaucracy. So we set sights on Albany. And we arrived to find out that the politicians in the capital of the State of New York were in the pocket of Javier DeSantana.

He had an eerie presence when I first met him, like the pictures I'd seen of the voodoo Loa Baron Samedi, the taker of souls. That aside, Javier was at the height of fashion, just as he is now, and he had a long cane with a jeweled tip, a center ruby ringed with diamonds. And he invited me to play chess.

We played, and we decided that my crew could run the streets with the lowlifes and degenerates, and we'd give Javier a very small cut. However, the cut wasn't much, but Javier wanted favors too. Extortion, stalking, sorting people out a bit and one time, a hit. He wanted to play gentlemen and let us do the dirty work.

So why the beef? Why the turf-war? Why else, that's why. We're criminals. Javier, in all his cashmere suits and refinements and chess-playing, was a petty con-man in a Jamaican prison not ten years before I met him. And me? I'm just a smarter thug than the other thugs that run with me.

I have his king in a hook with my knight. His queen's on the other end of the hook. She better be good. She better be Lucas Brody.

Brody was a master forger. He could make licenses, Social Security Cards, Passports, any set of credentials you could want, and on rare occasion, counterfeit money that would fool anyone.

Javier held his head in his hands. He couldn't block the knight; he had to move the king. He turned over his queen, sighed. He muttered *fuck,* and moved his king. I then took his queen, and sure as shit, it was Brody.

My guy wrote down his name with the others. Javier groaned, and took my knight with his rook. George Sampson, a shady attorney. He'd be missed.

I brought my queen out next. It was the beginning of the end. I always did as much damage as I could with my knights and bishops before taking her out. When I would play Javier at our regular meetings, I'd bring out the queen first. I'd play like hell, but I knew I would lose. That's what you do when you're a little fish playing a bigger fish. You give them a run for their money, but you take a dive. That way they respect you, but don't feel threatened.

I had his rook and his king trapped. And my queen was on the warpath, taking out pawns, my guy scribbling down their names between moves. Javier was scrambling, but it was no use. My pawns were largely intact, I had a knight, a bishop, both rooks and my queen. He was down to a rook, his king and the pawns being picked off one-by-one.

It took five moves to get Javier into checkmate. He still had his rook.

"So it ends," He said, his eyes hollow, black skin moist from nervous sweat.

"So it does," I said. "Who's the rook, if you don't mind my asking?"

Javier didn't respond. He was in shock. I didn't need to know.

"Javier, this is it," I said. "It's time. As we agreed."

Javier could've refused to honor the rules. He might've been smart to do it too. He'd have stood a better chance. But his face required saving, a sort of pseudo-honor that by necessity bound him to his word. By reneging, he'd have lost all the same.

"As we agreed," he said.

Our guys went out of the trailer to the road to get a signal. They had to phone in all the hits.

Bad Samaritan

Her scream pierced the cold city night. Henry had the window opened; his apartment was the Sahara 'cause the super wouldn't fix the damn heat. He looked outside. Most, hell, all of his neighbors minded their own business when they heard trouble on the block below. They sure as hell did it when his wife was robbed and shot two years ago. There were people on the street, people in the buildings above. No one wanted to get involved.

He peered down, but the woman was screaming "Help me! Anybody please!" He'd had it with the place. He turned off the lights and went to the closet, where his liquor stash was. The door creaked, and he took out what would get him by – a Remington .308 bolt-action with a flash suppressor. He took position in the window-sill, backed up far enough to keep the barrel from peeking out the window. He sighted in, locating the man, who at this point was on top of the woman. He had a clean shot. He slid the bolt back, put one shell in, and in a fluid motion closed it. He sighted in again, flipped the safety. A center-mass shot might hit her – he'd have to pull a head shot. With one breath, he squeezed the trigger. He watched it just to see the flap of scalp pop off the top of the would-be rapist's head. There were witnesses, and there would be more.

...but they wouldn't want to get involved.

Carolina Reapers

I looked out over the flat grassy expanse, an acre
of land to be torn by the tractor, plowed, planted and
fertilized. The Southern California sun was pulling
sweat through my forehead, soaking the band of my
Stetson. I uncapped the plastic liter bottle of tap
water and took a swig. It was still cold enough to
send a replenishing sliver down my guts. I thought
of the diner in town, and the granite-faced tractor
hogs, or the Mexicans, and how they'd laugh at a
water bottle on a day under ninety degrees. But I
wasn't a farmer. In fact, I started my career at that
very same diner in the back as a short order cook.

I got a hundred acres from an old man named
Big Ted, who had a dream and a wish, and bags of
seeds. We lived twenty miles from each other, but
we met at a Chili cook-off in Abilene, Texas. I
brought my restaurant's award-winning chili, but
Abilene was the World Series that year. We didn't
even come close. Big Ted came in second to a grizzly
bearded Texan named Cyrus. Later that night I
went out and got drunk with Big Ted.

"He got his thing, boy," he said. "Got an ace. He's a mad scientists with his peppers."

"I thought yours was better."

"The hell it was, but thanks, Bill." Big Ted dropped the Genesee Cream Ale down his throat and called out for a refill. "He told me his secret one night, but I thought he was horsing me. I'm gonna tell you though. I don't have many years, maybe not another one." He burped.

"He feeds 'em meat." Big Ted whispered.

"What? The beef?"

"Nah, the seeds. The peppers, man. He got a hog farm, and he chips up five, six hogs and spreads it on the crop when he plants. It's the peppers."

"That's not illegal, is it?"

"Hell no, it's ingenious. Wish I listened to him."

Me and Big Ted got close before he passed on. He'd come to the restaurant with cuts of meat, ham so sweet I don't know what he was feeding them. I asked for his butcher, but he said something like "A man's gotta take some of his tricks to the dirt."

Big Ted was a hard man wrung through an even harder life. A child of the Depression, he spent hours on end sharing his stories, as we sat on the faintly sagging front porch of his farmhouse. He showed me the canvas tent he and his mother lived called home in Biloxi in the thirties, spoke of heat and hell on an island called Peleliu during World War Two, and every decade since his life was one prize-fight after another. But Big Ted had found a place in Americana, a time of drive-in diners and apple pie, picket fences and bake sales, and he set himself there. The modern era confused him some.

One day, Big Ted grabbed himself a moving van and took off to do the year's chili circuit. I was stuck at the restaurant, trying to keep it afloat as the recession dragged on. It was two years before Big Ted walked in and got a seat at my bar.

"You win anything?" I said.

"Naw, just gettin' tips," he said. "Got some meats too. I'm gonna' try it like Cyrus done."

"Well, if you need my help, Ted."

Ted coughed. I could see a spot of blood in the napkin.

"I may need more than your help," he said. He tossed a sealed letter on the counter with a coffee-cup ring stain on it. "Open it Saturday. Not a day before."

Ted ordered a Scotch and threw it down, ice and all. He wiped his lip with his hand and his hand on the strap of his overalls and he walked out the door without another word.

Of course, I opened the letter on Friday night. Couldn't help it. It was hand-written, neater than I'd have figured for Big Ted. I read in astonishment.

Bill,

If you read this before Saturday, don't come by. Nothing you can do to stop me. I got no family, and where I'm goin'...won't matter how I get there.

Long Pig ain't bad. That's human meat, you know. That stuff I brought over, said was pig. Long Pig, that stuff...

Cyrus was a tough boar to put down, but I did. And I got five more on the circuit. Don't worry, you ain't been fed circuit folks. That's what Cyrus done. He used vagrants. Ain't no real hogs feedin' his peppers.

You're a good man, Bill. A good friend to an awful S.O.B.. When we were at the market one day, I wrote out an IOU, remember that? Probably not, but I put the farm as collateral. I don't have a cent to my estate, and I'm willing you my place. It's a hundred acres. Just promise me one thing.

In the shed out back, the one I kept my freezers in, you'll find the map to one clear acre. In the fridge, you'll find the fertilizer. Now don't worry, I prepared it. It looks like shredded jerky. The yellow and orange bags got enough seeds for the acre. They're good peppers, Bill. Real good peppers called Carolina Reapers. Two-point-two million Scoville Heat Units! Be careful, buddy.

No one will come calling about the fertilizer, I made sure of it. I'm leaving it to you. Make something good of me, Bill.

The sun doesn't feel so hot now. Maybe I'm adjusting. I look over at the tractor. The plow's attached, and I have two hundred seedlings growing in the big barn. By this summer, I'll have the full acre planted.

Big Ted asked to be cremated in his will. I took care of it. You should always have some ash in your fertilizer.

Hopefully, I'll be bringing Big Ted with me to Abilene next year.

Game Time

"Full boat," Jo-Boy said, "bitches and sixes." He splayed out the queens and sixes with all the suave of a Vegas wannabe. His white wife-beater, if you could call it "white," was stained down the middle with a spray of blood. He'd offed Mitch's partner a half-hour ago. They were in the break-room of an abandoned warehouse on Lincoln Ave. Secluded; that's why they picked it.

Maria's cries would periodically interrupt the game. Maria was Mitch's girl, and they had her. Now the dregs of Marco's gang, Johnny Sip, Jo-Boy and Vince Marco, the boss's reject nephew, played the game as Mitch shuffled his cards. They had their guns on the table, barrels all pointed at him.

Mitch loved it when people went out of their way to intimidate someone. They always left themselves open. They were slugging Bacardi 151. Mitch declined, citing that he was a Mormon. They spent the past hour slugging the fire-water in front of him and, until a half-hour ago, his partner. He might have been offended, if he really was a Mormon. He just needed to keep his edge, and encourage them to lose theirs. He passed the cards to Vince to cut, and he dealt them.

Ace high. Shit else; he'd have to hope for a magic draw, or the action would be starting at the end of the hand. He added twenty to his ante, and that made the rest of them just check.

"Got something good there, Mitch?" Vince asked.

"Spectacular," he said. Then he discarded the remaining four and held up his ace. They all laughed.

"Twenty bucks on an ace. Dumb motherfucker," Johnny Sip said. "I can beat you sleeping."

That got a whole bunch of laughs. Vince took two, Johnny took one and Jo-Boy took three. Mitch dealt everything out. He came up with a pair of aces, nothing to win with. It was game time.

"All in" Mitch took three-hundred dollars out of his wallet and opened the flap, showing them. He tossed it in the pile. They may have suspected something, but they were so drunk that all they suspected was a big bluff. Ricky went all in, and when he lost, Jo-Boy put a bullet in him.

"Oh, you got balls," Johnny said. "I'll go all in with ya'... You know what happens if you lose, right?"

"Oh yeah."

"Maria's gonna look good on the web."

Mitch didn't respond. He just laid out his pair of aces.

"You got a fuckin' death wish, Mitch?" Johnny asked. He laid down two pair, kings and tens.

"Motherfucker!" Mitch yelled and flipped over the table with a speed they couldn't match being drunk. As they were getting their bearings back, he took the table legs and flipped it one more time, throwing it in their direction. The guns were on the floor in front of him. He picked up Jo-Boy's .38 Special and Vince's .45 and stood up, crossing his arms to plug Johnny in the head and Jo-Boy dead center in the chest. He trained both guns on Vince.

"Be careful of what you do next," he said. Vince had a complete look of shock on his overgrown face.

"Take me to Maria right now, and I'll let you live."

"O-okay," Vince said, "she's upstairs. Just chill."

"Take me there, and move slowly," Mitch said. "I want to see your hands the whole time, you hear me?" Vince nodded, and they went to the stairwell.

"Johnny...Jo-Boy..."

"You wanna' play mobster, Vince, you better learn not to get attached to your cohorts. You see me whinin' over Ricky?"

"B-but..."

"Fuck you, Vince. Just move." Maria's cries were intensifying. She must've thought they killed him. He listened for the sound of anyone else in the room with her, but he trusted his earlier intel'. Those three were the only ones in the building. They were the ones that were supposed to be guarding her.

If they knew what Mitch's real name was, Marco would've had the place crawling with thugs. They got to a steel door, and Vince went to open it. Mitch stopped him. He motioned Vince in front, and banged on the door.

"Maria, they're dead! I'm coming in to get you." He waited for a second, just in case some unforeseen thug was in there prepping to pop him when he opened the door. Then he threw it open with one hand, shoving Vince inside with the other.

Nothing. He could see the light, and he swept through the doorway, .45 aimed. No one; Just Vince, and a sorry-looking Maria, tied to a bed.

"That'll be all, Vince," Mitch said. As Vince turned to walk out, Mitch put a slug in his calf. He dropped in the doorway and screamed.

"Asshole!" He said. "You said you wouldn't shoot me!"

"No," Mitch said as he untied Maria. "I said I would let you live." He pulled an untraceable cell-phone out of his pocket and tossed it to Vince. "Call 911. You don't want to let yourself bleed out, do you? Because then it's on you, not me."

He freed Maria, and they stepped over Vince.

As they made their way out of the warehouse, Mitch pulled out another untraceable cell and started dialing.

"Who are you calling?" Maria asked.

He finished dialing and hit *send*. As soon as he did, the warehouse flashed as an explosion rattled the whole block with the shockwave. The windows exploded in the flames.

"Vince."

Don't Blow It

"Shoot him!"

JoZee paced the blood-spattered concrete floor of
the old slaughterhouse on West Street. The room
stank like stale cigarette smoke and fresh piss.
Jerome was duct-taped to a steel folding chair, his
face spent the past half-hour french-kissing the butt
of Paolo's Glock.

"Shut the fuck up, Joe..."

Paolo took off his wife-beater, tossing it to the
floor. He got up close to Jerome. Jerome Sanders;
that's what it said on his name-badge when they took
him. Some fancy company in the new executive
park; *Sentinel Biotech.* He didn't much care for
where the guy worked, what he did, or what his
favorite wine and cheese were. Paolo just cared
about the briefcase chained to the guy's arm, the
combination on it, and the contents that Jerome was
dealing on his turf.

He had people deal on his turf before. A show of
the heat, a punch in the face - that was the usual

course of action. At least those clowns were selling real shit. This guy was selling bogus blow. Paolo's customers were leavin' for the PJs. He didn't want to get into the briefcase for the *drugs;* he wanted to shove the bags of bullshit powder down Jerome's throat to let him choke on it. But he wouldn't talk, just kept coughing.

Paolo slammed Jerome's chained hand on a thick wooden table and put a round through his palm. The impact jerked his hand up before the pain could do it. Jerome screamed out, started coughing like gangbusters.

"Yo, he's gonna' die, homes." JoeZee said.

Paolo leaned in close to Jerome's swollen ear. "Not if you give me the combo to your briefcase, motherfucker." Then he swung the barrel across Jerome's face.

"Alright! Fine! I'll *cough* give it to you... *cough*" Jerome said.

Paolo smiled. He grabbed the briefcase and slid it on the table. "Go. And no tricks."

Jerome coughed and hacked. "Two... *cough* ... seven... *cough*..."

"Go on... You can do it. Two more left, and you'll be free."

"*cough* Four... *cough*... zero."

Paolo slid the combo, and the briefcase popped open. It was lined with big, sealed bags of powder. It didn't even look like coke. *Must've been why he dealt at night.*

He picked up a bag and tore it open flinging the powder all over the place. He traced his finger along the inside of the bag and rubbed the residue on his gums. *Nothing.*

"You gonna' sell this fake coke on *my block*!?" Paolo screamed. He grabbed another bag. "Before I cram all this shit down your throat, you got any last words?"

Jerome hacked. He blew out a bloody snot bubble.

"Yeah..." Jerome said before he threw blood up onto his already-soaked shirt. "I'm dying."

Paolo laughed. "You don't say..."

"...*cough*... So are you... and your friend." He pointed with his bloody stump-hand to the bag in Paolo's grip. "That's not coke."

"Oh yeah?" Paolo said to JoeZee, "Listen to this guy! So tell me, *Jerome,* what *is* in these bags?"

"*cough* Druggie killed my wife... *cough*... So I faked a shipment from... *cough*... Level 4, where I work... *cough*... worked. Sold it on your street as coke... *cough*..."

"What is it!?" JoeZee asked. He cleared his throat, the dust was still in the air.

"*cough* *Bacillus anthracis...* "

JoeZee grabbed Paolo's arm. "That last word sounded like-,"

"Anthrax...*cough*," Jerome gasped. "Pneumonic...*cough*... *weaponized.*"

Jerome slumped over in the chair. Paolo let out a cough.

Black Cat Bone

Billy's jacket collar was soaked in sweat as he stood outside the Fourth Street Market, waiting for Hawkeye to buy a case of Miller High Life, the 'Champagne of Beers'. They usually went for whatever would leave them money for an extra pack of smokes, but the day was good. The cops had other shit to do that morning, and they got a good four hours on a Sunday squatted strategically on the corner of Third and Liberty, where St. John's Church was laying down some 'give to the poor' sermon and everyone had to pass by to get to the parking lot.

They cleaned house on Sundays, going from church to church from nine until one. Hawkeye wouldn't tell him the take, he never would, but he promised to come out with two packs and a case. He spotted Hawkeye's burly olive jacket, likewise soaked, with a case of the High Life and a bag. He grunted and tossed Jimmy a pack of generics and a fat piece of teriyaki beef jerky. Lunch.

"Let's get," Hawkeye said. They started walking their spot under the bridge across the Hudson River. It wasn't home. The only home either of them had were the jackets they were wearing. The jackets they wouldn't take off, not even in August. He wondered how many people knew that when they were catching coin on the sidewalks, they were working from home. Both Jimmy and Hawkeye had everything, every little tool they needed stashed in a jacket pocket somewhere. Hawkeye even had an mp3 player, but it was busted.

Jimmy couldn't figure why he kept it, but there was a lot about Hawkeye he couldn't figure. All he knew was what happened to young, delicate guys like him on the streets, and that Hawkeye was Jimmy's keeper. His brother. He didn't act like it sometimes, but Jimmy knew Hawkeye would take care of him. If only he didn't hold out so much.

They sat under the bridge, looking at the river below the concrete wall. They were into their beers, and Hawkeye leaned over.

"I'm gonna get out of here, ya' know," he said.

"Right now?"

"No, I mean I got a way out," Hawkeye said, "I found a treasure."

Jimmy cocked his head. "What kind of treasure?"

Hawkeye laughed phlegm. "Wouldn't you like to know, Pin-Doll."

"C'mon, man," Jimmy hated Hawkeye's nickname for him, "I'm not gonna fuckin steal it. I just wanna see."

"Fine." Hawkeye opened his jacket and reached in. Jimmy saw a bone joint covered in dirt, a long bone, by how wide it was. It was just jutting out of Hawkeye's pocket.

"See?" Hawkeye said.

"It's a bone," Jimmy said, "how is that a treasure? Is it human?"

"Yup'." Hawkeye said. "But it's gonna' be my black cat bone." He pulled it all the way out and gripped it tight in his two concrete fists. "It's gonna get he the hell out of this shithole."

"That's too big to be a cat bone, black or other."

"Naw, pin, it's like that song. *Hoochie Coochie Man.*" Jimmy stared dumb. "Ain't you never heard a' Muddy Waters?"

"No, he a folk singer?"

"Blues. A bluesman. He's a goner for years, but he wrote about the black cat bone, and the mojo too. I'm sayin' it's a good luck hoodoo thing."

"Don't you mean 'voodoo'?" Jimmy said.

"Voodoo's that fake, commercial stuff," Hawkeye said. "Hoodoo is the real shit."

They both eye-fucked Hawkeye's hoodoo treasure.

"How?" Jimmy looked at the whole bone. It was long and thick, maybe a leg-bone, but Jimmy wasn't a bone guy.

"Don't you pay attention to anything, Pin?" Hawkeye said, letting one hand off to slam the remaining half of his sixth High Life. "That rich kid, the missin' kid? The flyer's up on all the stores we get our shit from. You never see anything, Pin. But I do. That's why I got my nickname. Not from stickin' bobby pins through my nose."

If Hawkeye didn't have a hundred pounds on him, Jimmy would've punched him in the face. But he did what he always did – clung on and played lackey.

"So that's the bone from the kid?"

"Yeah, Pin," Hawkeye said. "And there's a twenty five gee reward for information as to his whereabouts. That's the treasure."

Jimmy finished his sixth beer and reached in the case for another. "So you have the bone. Won't they want the rest?"

"Yeah, numb-nuts, but I know where it is," he said. "So all I got to do is call 'em, tell them I know where he is and show them my proof." He slugged into number seven, "They want to know the rest, I get twenty-five gee and I show them."

"What if they think you killed him?"

"They got no proof," Hawkeye said. "And I got frequent flyer miles at the County. I'll crash there until they sort it out, and walk out with twenty-five gees."

They drank on until there were only three bottles left. Boaters floated by on the river from the dam they couldn't go past, some with fishing poles and others with beers better than High Life. The sun was harsh that day, but under the overpass, Jimmy watched the shadows on the concrete grow fat. He figured out how to tell time that way. Actually, Hawkeye figured it out, but Jimmy was the one to ask.

The sun had set, oranges bleeding their intensity to the blues and indigos of the coming night. Hawkeye was walking around under the bridge, pretending he was a caveman, swinging the bone like it was a sword. Jimmy got up, feeling flushed and beautiful.

"Let me hold it for a second," Jimmy said, "I've never held a bone before."

Hawkeye tapped him on the shoulder with the jointed tip. "No way." He spun around, this time like a Shaman dancing to heal the sick weeds growing through the concrete.

"C'mon, Hawkeye. Not like I'm gonna take it. It's yours."

Jimmy stared dumb-faced as Hawkeye went to hand him the bone. As Jimmy reached for it, Hawkeye whapped him in the face. He wasn't ready for it, and he walked into it eyes open. Some dirt from the bone got in his eye, and he hunched over, his hand rubbing his eyelid. "Asshole. Why'd you have to do that?"

"You're such a whiny bitch, you know that? You're on your own when I get my cash, you know. I'm not taking some clinger with me out west when I-"

Jimmy grabbed an end of the bone. Hawkeye smiled, thinking it was a joke, and pulled it back, but Jimmy held fast. They went back and forth, wound up on the ground, wrestling with it. Then Jimmy heard the crack.

They both got up and each had half the bone. It had fractured down the middle.

"You little Nancy bitch!" Hawkeye said. He flipped the bone and swung it at Jimmy, hard as he could. Jimmy's face spun sideways, but he didn't hit the dirt. Maybe something was broken, but could bone break bone? His face filled with rage, and without flipping his bone shard, he lunged to stab Hawkeye is his namesake eye.

If Hawkeye was his height, Jimmy might have succeeded in nailing him in his eye. But Hawkeye was near a foot taller. Hawkeye staggered back, grasping at the bone shard embedded in his neck. He pulled it out, and blood sprayed, lub-dub with his heartbeat, which after a few seconds was slowing down. He had his hand at his throat, but that was little use – the blood spurted between the slits of his fingers. Hawkeye hit the ground and, in moments, there was no pressure in his veins to make the blood spurt.

Jimmy sat down, reached into the bag and picked up the beers, drinking them one by one until they were as dead as Hawkeye. Jimmy picked up both bone shards. It was his. The treasure, twenty five large that could get him the hell out of the shithole. He tucked them in his inside jacket pocket, the one with the bottom ripped, and left, heading for the nearest convenience store with a flyer.

Jimmy came to two realizations at once when he turned the corner by the Sheriff's Office. Hawkeye never told him where the body was. He killed

Hawkeye. If he wasn't so drunk, he would've realized that the second epiphany was more important than the first, but instead he spent the cool night stomping Hawkeye's haunts, digging through weeds as the moon shone just bright enough to make him know he'd never find the kid's bones. Maybe Hawkeye hid them?

Jimmy had the bone tucked in his coat walking down the street. He saw the bank clock read nine-twenty. Then it hit him: Any information about his whereabouts. He had the kid's leg-bone maybe. It proved he was dead. That was information. He would get the twenty-five gees either way. He made it to the nearest store, memorized the number and went to the payphone on First Street. He was sober by then.

"Detective Malloy," the voice said on the other line, "How can I help you?"

"Yeah, I'm calling about that kid, the one on the flyers. There's a reward for information?"

"Yes, there is." Detective Malloy said. "Do you have any?"

"I do, but I want to make sure I get that reward."

Silence on the other end.

"How about this? How about you come to the station tonight and tell us what you know. We have the reward right here."

"And you're sure you have the reward?"

"Yes, the family left it with us. I promise you, if you have the information, you'll get the reward."

Jimmy walked into the lobby of the police station and told the desk sergeant who he was there to see. He waited until a squat, balding man with a bristling mustache came downstairs. He introduced himself as Detective Malloy, and led Jimmy to the elevator for the third floor.

"Wanna take your coat off?" He said.

"No thanks." Jimmy said. "I'm on the streets, I'm used to keeping it on."

"Okay, fair enough." Malloy guided him to a seat next to his. His desk was cluttered with paperwork.

"Ok, so, what information do you have regarding Gary Phillips?"

"Oh, that's his name?"

"Yeah."

"I can tell you that he's dead." Jimmy said.

Malloy cradled his chin in his hand. "And how do you know this?"

Jimmy pulled the two sections of bone from his coat. He put them together and placed them on the desk. Malloy's eyes grew.

"And this is his what, leg bone?" Malloy said.

"Yes. I don't know what happened to the rest of him. But you can DNA test it, right? I mean, if it's his leg bone, certainly he's dead, right? Blood loss and all.."

Malloy picked up the bones, smelled them, took the two shards apart and examined each.

"This certainly is information." Malloy said.

"So I get my reward money, right?" Jimmy was mentally on the bus, hell, maybe even the plane, heading for anywhere he wanted. Away from here.

"Well, I just have one more question for you." Malloy said.

"Oh, yeah...You'll need my name, right?"

"That," Malloy said, "And, since he disappeared a month ago, you might want to tell me why the blood on this bone shard hasn't even dried yet."

My Best Friend is a Ghost

"You ain't got the sand…" Floyd said as I caressed the .45 like a femme fatale.

"Someone's gotta' do it." Punk went by *Marley,* dreadlocked scum; probably hadn't taken a bath since his namesake died. He'd choked three of his *girls* for holding out on him, and they were just that; girls. The oldest, Cherise, was sixteen.

"Ya know, he'll get back at ya'."

"Him and every other ghost I fuck with." I said. "Not worried about it."

"Hey, I didn't fuck with ya," Floyd, hands up, smile on his face. "I came with the house."

"You know what I mean."

Floyd lit up a smoke "I'ma' sayin' there's other means."

I could hear the hood in the distance, shouts and cat-calls, blasting speakers, the thump-thump of frame-rattling car-speakers. I lived out in the sticks for a reason. I lived alone, not counting Floyd. But Cherise came to me with ligature marks. The other two had passed. She couldn't. Floyd told me to get out of Dodge about the whole thing. But, being a ghost, he didn't attract ghosts. If he had, he'd have listened to the ghosts of a hundred other horse thieves back in his day and would've gotten out of the *real* Dodge. Shot dead in the street, he was.

I was in Kansas City, Kansas-side, Floyd in the passenger seat. He loved road trips. After spending a century stuck haunting a house in Dodge City, being able to latch onto me and go anywhere gave him good reason to like road trips. But on this one, he said stay home. Guess he must not have liked KC back then. I looked to see my cardboard pine-tree air freshener move on its own. Well, not really...

"Floyd, what're you doing?"

"I'm showin' ya what ya' can git' from a ghost," he said.

"Can I get you to make that thing smell again?"

"Depends on the smell yer' goin' fer'." Floyd said.

"So what? I send a ghost after him? Trip him to death with air fresheners, or broken plates?"

"I ran across one ghost that could do far more than that. You met him too, when you was little."

"Who?"

"Your first haunt. The boogeyman in your closet."

"No. Not him." I said.

"He'd be perfect."

"He was, and is, evil," I said. "He didn't miss the light... he shot at it."

"..and you could toss him into it if you wanted to."

I thought about it. Quantrill was his name, though saying it would bring him... hell, he may as well been in my back seat by just thinking his name. William Quantrill was the evil behind the Jesse James gang in the Civil War. Quantrill didn't like me much, and the feeling was mutual. But Floyd had a point; Quantrill's spirit could blow an axle on a car and send it careening toward Marley.

"Floyd, I'd either have to unleash him in a populated city, and if I unleash... him... on KC, where will he stop?"

"I'll stop when my own personal business is done." I heard a gritty voice from the back seat. *Quantrill.* I looked back to see piercing eyes and a handlebar mustache peeking out of his bushwhacker hat, grimy as his voice. Jesus, he was scary. Floyd froze. Even other ghosts were scared of him.

"How did you get out of Lawrence, William?" I asked calmly.

"I hitched a ride, son," he said. "You drove right by on your way here."

"I won't release you here, William." I said.

"You think I'm gonna' tear the city apart?" Quantrill said, laughing. "It's an old city... been here, done that." He paused. "There was a prison, Missouri-side, that the Union held our women captive.. Anyhoo, they burned a part of it down, said it was an accident... killed a few gals near and dear, if you know what I mean."

"That land is mine," he said. "Drop me off, I'll take that ornery bull ya' got out to pasture. Course, you could send me back to Lawrence, but I'll just take it out on the good folk of Lawrence..."

"...or I could toss you through." I said.

"... and I grab Floyd on the way out," he said. "Wasn't dumb in life, and still not dumb."

He could grab Floyd; he had a point. For some reason, I trusted Quantrill at his word on this one. I knew his history; he was right. There was a prison. I just hoped it wasn't a playground now, or a senior citizens' complex. He was going to make people suffer - did it matter where?

I opened my glove box, and pulled out my coin collection. I found a gold coin. I flipped it in the back seat. Quantrill faded and the coin lit up red for a second. I put the .45 away, and drove to the block that Marley hung out on.

He was sitting on the steps, hustling teens to horny older men for petty scratch. I pulled up, taking the warm coin off the back seat. It was in mint condition. Hopefully Marley was smart enough to take it, if only to rob him.

Marley walked up. "Yo, what you need?"

"I need a date."

"How much you got?" He asked.

"I got this." I handed him the coin. "It's a fifty-dollar gold piece from the 1860's. Worth about five-thousand now. That's all I got."

Marley looked it over. Then he handed it back. *It was cold.* "Nah, man... Cash only."

I took off. Quantrill was on Marley now. And I didn't lose my coin. I still felt like a death-broker.

Floyd looked at me, rubbed his chin. "You wanted to pass him through, huh."

"Yeah."

"Sorry, hombre... I shouldn't have tagged along."

I looked over as we made our way out of the ghetto. I sighed.

"What can I say? My best friend is a ghost."

The Fear

The old man cut high-and-tights in a store-front barber-shop, original pole and everything. He was old-school; straight razor shaves and hot towels and horse-hair brushes with the lathering soap, he talked the day's news with the other old fucks that haunted his shop. Some of them knew; some of them didn't. But aside from a shave-and-a-cut, the only time I ever talked to him was when he flipped the *open* sign to *closed* and my barber went back to being my boss.

He was tied to New York. My last boss was a penny-ante franchise, but the old man was a "Family" man. He caught a Jazz concert at Lincoln Center every two weeks – I probably couldn't point it out on a map. I didn't care where he really went; never asked. Wasn't my business. I was muscle. I was the fear that gave the old man his power up here. I was the voice that haunted degenerates, the fists that brought blood to the mouths of those who didn't make good on their agreements.

I remember the day the old man brought me into the mess that got me out of the game. It was cold as fuck outside and it took me two whole minutes to warm up in the barbershop.

"Rick, have a seat," said the old man. "I need a favor."

I sat down on one of the barber chairs, not relaxing, mind you, just sitting. I'd come to learn that *favor* was another word for 'headache' in this game.

The old man paced the floor. His guys in New York weren't terribly impressed with his *management style*, so was word on the street. He was getting desperate to throw up revenue, and desperate people get stupid, no matter how smart they are when they're not desperate.

"There's a couple of kids, got another operation going," he said. "They came to me about it."

"You got names and addresses?" I wondered how deep the punishment would be.

"Oh, no, nothing like that," The old man said. "They got a guy out there, owes them fourteen. They can't get it out of him, so they came to me to help them collect. They get pennies on the dollar; we pocket the rest."

Taking on amateur two-bits? Collecting someone else's debt? Now, I know what you're thinking. Well, I know what *I* was thinking. But as I said: I'm muscle. I'm fear. I'm not *common sense.*

And I don't give what I don't get paid for. So the old man invited me to dinner to meet these clowns. The old man wanted to flex muscle, impart fear. For that, I got paid.

Dinner at Corrazo's was held in a back booth. The old man and I sat on one end, and the sandbox bookies sat on the other. I had steak, medium rare, and the old man had linguini with clams. The kids ordered lobster and filet mignon. What kind of assholes order the most expensive shit on the menu when the check's covered by the guy they're asking for help? Were they trying to look cool or something?

Anyways, they talked. The old man was aiming to take their operation over, but it was a shitty operation at that. It was all text-based, and they didn't even try to keep low-pro, all dressed in the latest kiddie fashions. All this hoopla for fourteen-thousand. I collected on fifty more than once under the old man. Was he going senile?

The old man nodded with his fork towards me, indicating that I'd be the one saving their scrawny asses.

"Are you a cop?" One of them asked. "I mean, it's cool if you are.."

It took every ounce of juice not to laugh in his face. I looked at the old man. He nodded for me to answer him.

"No." I said, and continued eating my steak. I said it cold. I didn't want them to trust me. I was only aiming for fear.

So needless to say, I had a fourteen-thousand dollar debt to collect for a bunch of wannabe's and a desperate boss. So I collect. I go to the guy's house, ring the bell and he answers.

"You owe some money," I said, "and your debt's been passed on to me."

"Look, man," The guy said. "I'm broke right now. I can get you some of the money when I get my check, but I gotta' go to work tomorrow. It's late."

You might be expecting a baseball bat and some blood, but no. There's a technique to fear. Inflict violence at the first brush-off, you just make 'em angry and uncooperative. So I try a different approach.

"What time do you go to work tomorrow?" I ask calmly. I know where he works; not important.

The guy was surprised. "Uh...nine o'clock," he said.

"Here's what's gonna' happen," I said, again, calmly. "You're gonna' meet me at Joe's at seven o'clock tomorrow morning, before you go to work, and we'll discuss what you owe."

"Okay," The guy said. "But I don't have any cash now."

"That's fine." I said. "Just meet me at Joe's, seven a.m., okay?"

The man nodded, and I told him to have a good night. And I left.

Collection is a mind game. Maybe he'd show, maybe he wouldn't. And this is all about anger and fear. I come at you angry, you go on the defensive, maybe do something stupid like buy a gun and put me in the sights. You may not have the grip to squeeze on me, but it doesn't make my day better. But you give a guy the impression that you're reasonable, *professional,* show him that you have trust in his integrity; he disobeys that trust, and you're anger is justified; it's *expected.* And that expectation is the fear. That's the control.

But, seven a.m. sharp, the guy's sitting at the back table. I slide up, make nice, order a coffee and bacon and eggs. If he's wired, it might be my last meal on the outside.

I got to it.

"Ok, Jack," I said, "From now on, you're gonna' be dealing with me about this." I slid him the number to my burn phone. "If anyone comes to you about this, call me. I'll take care of it."

He took the number and tucked it in the pocket of his flannel shirt.

"Now, you owe fourteen thousand dollars." I said.

"Fourteen grand?" He whispered. "I only borrowed eight grand, and I was supposed to pay back eleven. And I paid those other guys five hundred regular until last week. So I'm down to six."

I've heard plenty of jaw from people about how they don't owe what we say they owe. I hear it so much I can tell 'em what they're gonna' come up with before it clears their voice-box. That's 'cause we don't fuck around with our books.

Trust goes both ways. We trust they'll pay; they trust we won't screw the terms up. But this is another operation's debt. All bets were off. And the guy wasn't putting me on; I could tell he was being straight.

"Look," I said between sips of coffee. "I'll talk to my guy about that, but I can't promise nothing. It's not my department. But, if you're right, and you may be, you still owe six. Now, I know you're strapped, but is there anything you have that you can sell? Just a good faith thing, show that you aren't brushing off the debt, you know?"

Jack thought about it. "I got a big-screen TV, fifty-two inch, still in the box. I just don't know who'll buy it on short notice."

"How about this; I'll meet you after work. I'll take the TV and use that to take off some of your debt. It doesn't sound like much, I know how much they go for, but with this, it'll get ya' three hundred off your debt."

"Just three hundred?" Jack said.

"Fraid so," I said. "But it's a good faith thing. We'll know you're not brushing us off."

Jack agreed to part with the TV, and I brought a guy to help me put it in my van. The guy was one of the old man's guys. So we took it to the old man's house, a palatial little number up in the hills. First time I'd been there. Last time I'd want to.

The old man looked the TV over.

"What'd you take off?" He asked.

"Three." I said. "They go for twelve, so I figured three."

The old man scratched his head. "Fuck it." He said. "Three. Now how's he gettin' the other, what, thirteen-seven?"

"Ya know, I gotta' talk to you about that," I said. "I talked to him, and you know I been in the game a while. I get people tell me they don't owe what we know they owe, but this guy told me that he borrowed eight from those guys, which put it at eleven with the vig, and he paid them five. I got a feeling about this one. I think he's on the level about that."

The old man walked up to me so close I could smell the garlic in his sweat.

"He pays the thirteen-nine!" He screamed. "I don't pay you to think or to second-fucking-guess me, you got it?"

What the fuck? Oh, no, no, no...

"Listen here, motherfucker." I said. "I'm your *muscle.* You don't yell at people like me. You don't fucking *exist* without muscle. Don't you *dare* get up in my face again."

The old man looked like he saw a ghost. I don't think he ever got yelled at before, especially not by someone under him. I was ready to go; his guys had to pull me away. I didn't care. New York was coming up to oversee his shitty, crumbling empire and he had the stupidity of being a hired gun for nobodies who didn't know shit about loans. I'd been in other crews before; I knew the game. The old man was grasping at straws, and New York was looking to take a sip out of his old, wrinkly ass. That's when I knew I was out.

I never saw Jack again. And were it not for the day my mother got a visit from a man dressed in an ill-fitting suit asking where I was, I would've been out of the game forever. As it was, I'd been off-radar for two years before that prick showed up.

I walked into the barbershop one day. The old man wasn't there, but his good friend Wally was there and a few of his old muscle were still around, sitting on the waiting seats. Some gave me recognition, some gave me avoidance. Johnny looked up in surprise.

"Hey Rick," he said as his straight-razor went to work on a customer, one of the old man's associates from New York. "Didn't expect to see you here. Where ya' been hiding?"

"Haven't been hiding," I said, "Just out of the game, that's all."

"So, what've ya' been doing with yourself?"

"Relaxing." Rick said. "Until the old man sent someone to mom's house."

Johnny stopped the razor. "Oh, I don't know nothin' about that."

"I know," I said. "It's amazing how honest someone can be with their balls in a vice. Amazing how messy they can be too."

"Wait, Rick, I mean," He backed up. The goons perked up and leaned forward.

"Look, Johnny," I said. "No problems. Just give the old man a message for me."

"Okay, go ahead."

"If he sends any grief my way, or my family's way – I know where he lives, where his kids go to school, where his wife plays bridge and goes shopping…and in case he doesn't think I have the balls.."

I reached into my coat pocket. The folded up stack of papers: names, numbers, addresses – the floor-plan of his house and three pages that contained everywhere the old man went, what the old man did for one whole day; even when he turned off the lights to go to bed. I tossed the papers onto the counter. And I reached deeper in the pocket, grabbed the other things in a zip-lock to keep them from soaking through my little dossier.

"What the fuck is that?" Johnny looked through the crimson film coating the inside of the baggie.

I smiled.

"The balls." I tossed the bag on an empty chair and walked out of the old man's barbershop.

It's been years. Nothing from the old man, or his New York associates. Maybe they chalked me up as a loss, or a liability. But I think, in retrospect, I was, in the end, for myself, what I was for them once:

The fear.

Provenance

After my first hunt, I decided to make art from the carcass. Didn't have much of a taste for the meat, so I felt a little extra pressure to use every part. I cut a wide swath of skin from the mid-section, and I tanned it. Yeah, no shit. And it wasn't easy, not in a tub. Thanks much for my top-floor apartment!

Anyhow, I did a pretty good job, ending up with a pale *canvas* hide, which I wrapped around a frame with due difficulty. I needed paint, so I collected all of the fat and boiled it down. I cooked the meat outside until it was charcoal. I know it's a waste, but you need a lot of charcoal to mix with the fat for anything even closely resembling black paint. I dried the blood - which is not red after it's dried to powder, by the way, and I dried and ground up every organ I could. The bones were ground; they made a very good white. With a hodge-podge of colors, I painted a portrait of Big Ed, to whom I owed a debt I simply could not pay. It was he that sparked my interest in hunting.

I finished after many hours and many cigarettes and many, many cups of coffee. Pride swelled in me as I looked at a swell semblance of Big Ed, his bulbous, hardened features captured in layers of homemade paint. I knew that all the great works came with a *provenance*. Didn't know too much about what went into one, but that it was a document of the origin of the work. My masterpiece deserved a provenance. So I wrote it as best I could.

This work had its origin in a debt owed by me to you, Big Ed, for sending Tony after me and my family to collect. My wife nearly died, and to you, I now owe the pleasure of this artistry. You sent Tony, and I am now returning him to you. As I have glued this Provenance to the back of the painting, you are, at the moment, touching his skin.

If you feel the need to send someone else after me, please send Teke. He is a much larger, fatter man, and I need quite a bit of fat to produce the paint. I can also use a bigger canvas.

Enjoy your newly acquired work.

I didn't sign the Provenance. I wasn't sure if that's what you were supposed to do. By the time Big Ed figured out it was me who created it, I'd have the remaining scrap hides painted. I was thinking landscapes...

Unfinished Business

A Phoenix Tale

We lost the luster by the time I went in the Big' - '86, it was. We had an actor in the Oval Office trading firepower for hostages, so by that point, Reagan was getting more clout than *La Familia* when it came to shady shit. I got a quarter - twenty-five-to-life for making my sister a widow. Her husband's fists loved her face, and we all know one of em's gonna' go out the house in a black bag.

We gave him a Hefty bag, but it tore, and they used the piece left at the scene to match with the bag he was found rottin' in. I was nailed. I only got out in twenty-five because no one dared fuck with me in the Big, and I had a hell of a lawyer. And, the old DA passed on, and the new one couldn't be bothered to come all the way to Green Haven to protest. And my sis? She passed from cancer while I was in. She remained a widow, I mean, can ya' blame her?

I'm Benito Morretti now, not inmate number 013756. I used to be called *Bloody Bennie.* I was young, had a lot of venom that came out through the fangs of my matching, silver plated .44's. Wonder if Angelo kept those? Anyway, after I gave my first mook a trip to see Saint Pete, I was a seventeen-year-old kid. And I was a killer. You kill, you're a killer, and you make a decision in that first day, that first hour; fuck, that first second the life goes snuff.

You make it business, or you make it personal. No different with soldiers. Someone threatens their position, they blow heads off. *Business.* They get pissed and blast some civilian in the chest for flippin' 'em off; *personal.* You suffer and agonize over the personal ones. You repent; God will probably forgive you in the end. But business? No care, no agony, no torment; just a job and the review of all the t's crossed and i's dotted, a liter of Bourbon to numb yer' feet from the coals of that fiery road you're on.

Yeah, I'm goin' to hell. Do I deserve it? Yup'. Do I hate God, good church-goin' folks, puppies and kittens and baby seals? Nope'; fuck, I *go to church* every Sunday. Angelo makes me. And the church don't burn. Probably 'cause it's made of stone.

Angelo got me a job at the Phoenix. That was his joint when we were runnin' it up here. He kept it, but everything was hush now. Everything was business and forms and paperwork and invoices - not kickbacks for eyes going elsewhere and handshakes.

For the first time since I'd ever known it, the Phoenix was legit.

Father Walt from Saint Mike's was tending bar. He knew all the family secrets. He got hooked up with a woman from the parish, got caught with his pants down back in '66. Walt was a good ole' priest too, from talk about town. But he was an even better bartender, and wasn't he just taking confessions from drunks now instead of guilty Catholics? The Phoenix did serve wine. I suggested to Angelo that we serve crackers at the bar too. Angelo shot me a look...*that* look. So no on the crackers.

I was a fish out of water at first, when I got out, ya' know? I mean, protection was pointless - no one paid. We ran gambling and loan-sharking, but Angelo had that all insulated. Guys with little lists of guys. Fuck, if I owed Angelo a dollar, I wouldn't even recognize the kid who came to collect. Angelo said it was better that way. Little to trace back.

Prostitution? Meet crack. Yeah, I knew that shit was gonna' be bad when I went in. It was new then. Now it, and the hookers sellin' ass for it, was old. Only thing worth getting into was international, and Angelo told me about what that entailed. Didn't sound good to me either. But the real thing? Identity theft. That was the crime *du jour*. Kids behind computers. They didn't even *have* a web when I was barred from ever using one. I just learned email a week ago.

The old crew was a waste. Tommy Triggs, my second, my own muscle - blue suicide, but more likely, Tommy thinking a .357 Mag can top a SWAT team. Double-tap, death on spot, from what I heard. And Itchy? Always scheming crazy shit on Jim Beam and whatever hallucinogen he could get his hands on? Nut-hatch.

He believed he was a mobster. Which was true. But he also believed that Al Capone was guiding him from a book behind his eyeballs. I'm surprised he hasn't tried to escape "Alcatraz." And on and on the list goes; this one got popped, this one got shot, that one OD'd, the other guy went legit. Angelo, me and his new crew - that's what remained. But I had one piece of unfinished business. I had my nephew.

Benny Scorrelli - He has my first name, and a dead man's last name. And I made his last name worthless. That wouldn't change, even if Lisa took her maiden name. He'd always be a Scorrelli. And I got word he wanted to meet me.

I'm not sentimental towards a kid I last saw learning he had fingers. Well, a little. This kid was in his twenties, and he knew I killed his dad. Nephew or no, payback's something I had to expect. So I borrowed one of the Berettas Angelo had lying around. Numbers were scratched off nice and technical-like. I've been told forensics is the big growing industry. You can't just wing it like you used to.

I rode Angelo's old Chevelle to the address Lisa gave me before she died. It was a dingy apartment with a layer of neglect on the warped baby-blue siding. Garbage cans were out front - maybe someone should've told them that's where the garbage goes, as the shit was strewn all over the sidewalks. What happened to showing pride in your neighborhood? My dad would've whooped my ass with a strap if he came home from a day's work to see the city dump line his footpath. But I guess you can't take a strap to a kid these days.

I could smell reefer and hear a brat screaming as I knocked on the kid's door.

Who is it!? I got back as a reply. We used to put peep-holes in our doors for a reason.

"It's me, Bennie," I said. "Your uncle."

"Fuck off." Kid tells me. "Go away."

And he was the one that wanted to see *me.* He had a shit-lock and I pressed light against the door. No deadbolt. *Beautiful.* I slid out my library card (you learn to appreciate reading in the cage) and slid the lock. I had the gun in a shoulder holster under my jacket. Little Bennie, if he had a gun, wouldn't shoot me. Not at first. I'd have plenty of time to draw on him if I had to. But I wasn't there for gunplay. I love being free to fuck hookers and learn the new tricks of the family bizz. Plus all the newbies to teach.

I walk in, kid's sittin' on the couch and his hand slid under the middle cushion. I let the flap of my jacket out.

"Don't try," I said. "You'll hesitate. I won't. Got me?"

The kid sunk back down into the couch. The whole place was a mess. If Lisa was still alive, she'd be screaming bloody murder, and not at me. I dusted off the recliner and sat down. Wouldn't have sat down at all if I was wearing my good clothes.

"So you're gonna' kill me too now, right?" He said. "Finish the job, right?"

I sighed. "Bennie," I said, "roll up your sleeve for me, will ya'?"

"Which one?"

"Doesn't matter." I said. "They both look about the same."

Bennie rolled up his left sleeve, and I could still make out the faint marks, like plague scars.

"Maybe you wanted to know why all these years? Maybe you thought ma' was dumb or blind or something, visitin' me in the cage all those years. You never got to know me."

"I'm listening. Go ahead; tell me your sob story or whatever it is." Bennie said.

"Oh, you want a sob story?" I slid my hands down the arm-rest. "I got one."

"I had a sister once – Lisa. You knew her as mom." I started. "She was beautiful, and a good Catholic girl - in our family, we need those, cause a lot of us are gonna' be takin the *down* escalator. Anyways, she meets a guy; you knew him, briefly, as dad.

"He seemed like a good guy at the time, and I was really happy for them both. We put on a hell of a wedding. And when you were born, you wanted for nothing. Any expense was covered."

I have to admit, the next part was tough for me. Granted, Bennie was bein' a punk, but this wasn't even for his benefit - it was for mine.

"Then she comes into your uncle's hotel with a shiner." I continued. "Said she walked into a door. A lot of that happened back then - clumsy women walking into doors or falling down the stairs - no one at the hospital said anything about it.

And babies rolled around in ashtrays; and that's where we get to the end of the sob story. I walked in unannounced one day. Lisa was washing you; you couldn't have been more than two. And I see the burns, the scars on your arms when they were fresh."

Bennie listened. He tried to be unmoved, but I had twenty-five years of seein' people act like something they weren't.

"I've been accused of many things, and never plead guilty. For that, I plead guilty. I'd give my life for sis, and I gave twenty-five years of it for both of you."

"I never knew that." Bennie said. His voice was choked.

"Bennie!" came a shrill voice from the bedroom. Out walked this twig-looking thing with a joint in one hand and Bennie's kid in the other. And I saw the bruises and scars...

***

I feel grey now, just like the cinderblocks and the paint on the bars in the county lock-up. You should've seen the cops' faces when I called 9-1-1 to report a crime I committed, waiting for them, calmly cradling my great nephew as they arrived. Angelo visited. He said he's adopting little Benjamin. Go figure? Another little *Bennie*. I'm sure you've figured out by now, I'm pleading guilty. I'm doing the *whole enchilada.*

But I *did* learn how to use email. Not too shabby.

The Best Fall Flora

"When the blue of the night.. meets the gold of the day. ..."

Bing Crosby's deep timbre echoed off the cracked-plaster walls of Walt's two-bedroom house in East Durham. He stared out the window. It was on the edge of autumn, and the leaves were only sparsely changing colors. Another three weeks and the road in front of his place would see the big-city leaf-peepers driving through the Catskill Mountains like convoys through the photographic offensive. The perennials Sue planted still stood tall. It wouldn't be long before the first frost killed them all off completely for the winter, only to poke up anew in the spring.

"Perennials aren't the prettiest flowers in the world," Sue told him, "But you take care of them, they'll last forever."

Being married to Sue for fifty years, Walt came to rely on her practical nature. She preferred durable to pretty, simple to exotic, hands-on to conceptual.

She was Walt's perfect counterpoint, for he was none of those. Walt was sharp-dressed, flamboyant, wanted to see the beauty for beauty's sake. The first and only time he bought Sue a dozen roses, she ground up the flowers to make a folk remedy. Within six months, they were engaged. Their wedding was a small, family and friends in Saint Mary's Sacred Heart Church down the road.

Walt made a living as a writer; he was lucky. He found a niche in the hometown USA stories he wrote, and for decades he was prolific. But when Sue died, his work became dark. He was alienating his followers, including East Durham, Father McGinley showed up at his door one day.

"Sue loved your books, Walt," he said, "but what would she think of the new ones?"

Walt shrugged. "Don't know, padre," he replied. "She's not here to ask."

"Look, I don't care what people around here think, Walt. I know you, and this isn't dealing with your grief."

"Okay, what's God's plan for that? For that matter, about her getting hit by an idiot too busy snapping pictures of trees to see her on the edge of the road?"

Father McGinley rubbed sweat from his brow. "You used to take beautiful pictures of the foliage," he said. "You stopped doing it when Sue died. Why did you stop?"

Walt stared off.

"Is taking pictures dishonoring her memory because of how she died?"

Walt sighed. "Maybe, I don't know," he said.

"That's what I want you to do," Father said. "When you're ready, find the most beautiful scenery, and take pictures. It'll help you."

Walt took the father's advice. He went to the spots the leaf-peepers couldn't know about, the panoramas of the high peaks, fog like cumulous clouds embracing the river valleys before they rose off to work the crisp azure sky. But Walt deleted as many pictures as he took. There was nothing beautiful about any of it; nothing inspiring. It was what had always been.

He thought one day about a quote by Heraclitis; you cannot cross the same river twice. It amazed him when he first understood it. You couldn't cross the same river twice because the river is the water, and the water you crossed the first time has already gone away when you cross it again.

Maybe Walt's life was the river, and all the scenery in his lens was trying to cross it again. He had all but given up when he realized that there was something, a powerful thing that never had to cross the river because it was in the current.

So there Walt stood, remembering what Father McGinley said. He walked out of his house, turned, and walked to the road. He looked at them, and spun around. He aimed his camera at Sue's perennial garden, at the warm yellow-orange blanket flowers, clustered around the tall purples of Veronica and ringed with the light cherry-red Garden Flox. He adjusted his lens, backed up to get a better zoom, angled in and took the best shots of his life. He flipped through the camera to admire the most beautiful flora in the Catskills.

He felt such a wave of joy, he mistook the squeal of breaking tires for an eagle's cry.

Unlikely Memorial

It was a balmy night outside of the State Penitentiary of Texas at Huntsville. Daniel Rogers was going to fry at midnight. About a hundred pro-death-penalty protesters brought the noise, and another hundred anti-death-penalty protesters brought the light, as a hundred candles in vigil. Detective Jack Conlon was in the back, in his street clothes, arms wrapped around his biceps, a cigarette clasped between the two fingers of his right hand. Standing beside him was his partner, Ellroy Jacobs.

They watched the madness unfold in silence. Jack was asked to speak, by both sides, but he refused. *No comment,* he'd say to anyone who recognized him. He'd hunted Rogers for five years, ever since a case of three dead prostitutes with the same M.O.'s landed on his desk in Houston. He wasn't for or against the death penalty – if they could lock them up tight and never let them harm society again, he was fine with that. If they needed to die for what they did, so be it. He'd had to execute people in the line of duty; it was the same, minus the appeals. But Rogers plead guilty, and relinquished his right to appeal.

"You okay with this, Jack?"

Jack glanced over, took a drag of his cigarette. "I don't know yet."

Ellroy leaned back against a chain-link fence behind them. "We can always leave, if you want."

"No," Jack said, "I have to see this through." He tapped out the remains of his cigarette and flicked the butt.

"I understand if you want him to live," Ellroy said, "I can't hold it against you." Ellroy looked over at Jack, who had his hand at his brow, trying to gain his night-vision against the candle-light.

"He doesn't want to live," Jack said, "I can't argue with that."

"You should have never been on the case once they found out-"

"What?" Jack retorted, "That he was a stranger I'd never met in my life?"

"You know what I mean. After forensics got the evidence processed."

"It was personal when he started killing women, Ell'," Jack said, pulling another smoke out of his pack. "They all get personal after a while, you know that."

"I'm surprised the Chief didn't take you off it."

"I asked him not to," Jack said. "I knew the most about the case, and what we found out didn't change that." He paused. "...may have changed *me,* but it didn't change my case."

They stood around, quiet, as the clamor grew. At midnight, everything went hush. In any other case, Jack would've dropped a pin to see if he could hear it. But he flicked his latest cigarette butt instead. It hit the ground softly, but indeed he could hear it. About ten minutes later, the news came.

"At 12:01 a.m., Daniel Rogers was executed by lethal injection."

The crowd went wild in two directions. Jack and Ellroy let out a breath almost as one. Ellroy patted Jack on the back.

"So you're gonna pay for the body and bury him?" He asked.

Jack shrugged. "Yeah," he said, "I could give a rat's ass, but when mom found out who he was, she requested it." Jack turned to find the road out, Ellroy in tow.

"I hated the guy, but he *is* my half-brother." Jack added.

To Never Taste War

The Springfield jammed. That's what always broke his sleep – the constipated click of the trigger not followed by the explosion or the kick of recoil. He was powerless as the Mauser fire flew past, peppering the edge of the foxhole behind him.

Joe was slumped in the hole, eyes frozen open in an empty gaze. He'd been dead for three days. Thanks to the cold, no flies crept into his corpse; no smells of decay pervaded their position. K Company was bogged down, defending Wurlitz against an onslaught that had never been anticipated. God-damnit, he was cooking eggs on Monday.

The Big Red One had been captured, their supply line cut.

The convoys were out; no food or water, warm clothing or more importantly right then, ammo. He was running out. Aside from the bodily discomfort, he was still alive. That would change when he ran out of bullets. Until them, he would live with numb feet and the buzz of deadly lead mosquitoes zipping by his ear. He was just waiting for one to draw blood.

In the dream, he pried the Springfield out of Joe's icy grip. "Joe" wasn't his real name; they made it a point to make their formal acquaintances after they got out of that damned fox-hole. It was better that way. Names came with families, hometowns, hopes and dreams. They also came with obligations.

Harry took one of his dog-tags without looking at the real name. He tucked it in his pocket and went back to killing Germans. He'd killed a few, to be sure – he knew how to shoot. But killing a few in the presence of many wasn't anything to be proud of. *Killing* wasn't anything to be proud of. But he did just that. The rest of company K had positions around the town; some in the shelled, historic buildings, some around the densely-wooded perimeter.

It would be getting dark soon. The setting sun burned his retinas, though it didn't make him any warmer. It did make him stay low to squint out his targets He laid low, praying for night, when he could retreat under cover of darkness and try to regroup with his battalion; praying for rain to wash the snow away; praying the frozen ground wouldn't claim his feet. Praying he would live long enough to see at least one more sunset. It wasn't long before he took fire. And it wasn't but a moment after that that Joe's Springfield jammed.

In that long-ago acquired primal impulse, he reached under his bed as he woke up. He didn't often do that. When he returned from the War, he'd slept with a .45 under his bed. But that was thirty-five years ago.

He sat up, shaking. The sun wouldn't rise for another half hour. He blinked in the darkness, fumbling to reach the pull-cord on his bed-side lamp.

A lifetime working in a steel mill made him accustomed to getting up before dawn. It was ironic; he didn't even have to go to war because he worked at the steel mill back then. He went anyway.

He locked up the dream in the Pandora's Box of his mind and, laying his feet on the frayed carpet, opened his dresser drawer. A pack of Pall Mall's lay tucked under his whites. Smoking killed him, literally. Emphysema stole his energy and his breath, and smoking a cigarette came at a price every time he lit up. He'd more than once tried quit but he'd always had a pack, just in case. Just in case *Ardennes* came back.

He limped to the kitchen for coffee, pouring a cold cup from last night's pot. He drank it straight – cold suited him better right then. He took the coffee and his cigs and headed for the bar. Not really a *bar*, more a glorified breakfast nook. There wasn't any liquor. He quit drinking after nearly running his car over the Aqueduct.

It was a small bar. The trailer didn't have room for a *big* anything. Rita was still asleep, as she would be. Mary Anne would be stopping by with Liam later that afternoon. Of what little he could call his blessings, Mary Anne had given him a grandson. Seeing Liam would make up for the shitty dream.

He wasn't infantry. It's common knowledge that all soldiers in battle are there to fight, but in reality that wasn't the case. The blacks that drove the Big Red One were there to drive convoys. The office staff was there to push papers. His 103rd Combat Engineer Battalion was there to blow shit up for the bad guys, and rebuild it for the good guys. He was an engineer, and a cook. He wasn't infantry. Until the middle of December in '44, he wasn't doing much at all, just taking guns and equipment apart, cleaning them, and putting them back together. Christ, he could do it in his sleep.

They were defending a thirteen mile stretch along the Siegfried Line, where the Germans were pushed back. It was cold, and they stayed inside a lot, just posting the minimum on the front to look out. It was a no-battle battle-line. Then, on December 16th, the Germans advanced. Mortars started hitting Clarveux, where the 110th Infantry command was staying. Mortars were hitting everywhere. Then they started taking fire. Then came the SS Panzers. They were hopelessly outnumbered.

No one expected the Germans to hit there. In hindsight, it was the perfect place to hit. Harry's mind about that time was a patchwork of confusion and peril. He was forced to take one of the guns he'd spent so much time maintaining to go out and hold them off. Not just him, everyone had to fight: cooks, staff; hell, if the Army had clowns, they too would've had to go out there and sprayed lead through their oversized flowers.

They couldn't get air support because the winter cloud cover made that impossible. Later, he learned they were headed for Bastogne, and on to Antwerp, to capture the port. It was a long way to there, and Harry and the rest were the first stepping stone.

He sipped his coffee and sparked his smoke, leaning on his shoulders to keep his lungs from burning his chest. The Army he was once so fervent to join became the portrait of the demons the War gave him. He threw his medals away when he got back, and he never went to the VFW. He didn't need to be reminded of hell. Once he'd been there, he could never forget it.

When dawn poked through the windows of the trailer, he reflected. He did that in the War too, but under different circumstances. Dawn offered at least a few minutes of time to contemplate his life before it would be in mortal danger. Now, his contemplations were a habit. He thought of Mary Anne and Rita, the hell he'd put them through.

He found it easy to blame his harshness and temper on the War, but it made for an easy excuse, not a penetrating reality. There was something else in him, a demon he'd had since before combat. He couldn't name it. He called it alcohol, but quitting didn't banish it. He used to cruise the red-lights of Green Street in Albany when he was young, before he met Rita.

He was a gambler, and she never put her foot down, so long as he paid the bills and brought home a bucket of shrimp on payday. How often she must have prayed for him. He didn't pray much himself. Mary Anne was another story. She couldn't even live in the house until she was eight, he was so bad. Then all too quickly, she turned into a teenager, and rebelled.

They were distant. If he didn't have emphysema, he wondered if she'd even be bringing Liam to see them. To see Rita, for sure, but not to see him. Even when she did, they barely talked, like familiar strangers throwing about small-talk to break the uncomfortable silence.

He'd calmed down a lot since Mary Anne's upbringing. His demon was dying too. Sitting at the bar beat sitting in the dark in his bedroom for a week at a time, drinking coffee and smoking cigarettes. He remembered his mother not giving him an Easter basket when he was a kid because he didn't do something she asked of him. Is that why he wouldn't allow them to celebrate holidays? Is that why Mary Anne had to put a small Christmas tree in her room? The years made his memories blurry.

He made another pot of coffee and heard the thump of the paper hitting his door. He opened it up to a cold morning, hacked, and grabbed the day's news. He read it at the bar as he drank. Nothing interesting.

Jimmy Carter was elected president last year. *He wouldn't last two terms*, Harry thought, *too nice a guy*. He got a letter from Carter two days ago, hand-signed, commending his service in the War. He was going to chuck it, but he got distracted, and now he forgot where he'd put it. He'd get to it eventually.

He spent most of his morning on the Sports section, coming up with point-spreads for games. Football season was coming up; he'd have better luck with football games. He had a knack. Rita woke up, and he cooked her breakfast. They'd been married for so long that conversation was accomplished in a minute or less. She ate and took her place on the recliner after turning on the television.

Some people feared their marriage becoming a routine. They'd never tasted true chaos. Routine suited Harry just fine.

At noon, Mary Anne arrived with Liam in her arm. He was reaching out, smiling and laughing. Harry let her in.

"Hey, Dad," she said.

"Hey, Mary Anne."

"How are you feeling?" Liam reached out to him from her arms.

He pushed his hand to his chest. "The usual."

He knew she wanted to tell him to quit smoking. Had he been a better father, she would have.

"How's Liam?" He asked.

"He's doing good," she said, "he likes being naked."

Harry laughed, and then he coughed a bit.

"He's a kid," he said. "Nothing wrong with that."

She handed Liam over to him. She went to talk to her mom. That's how it usually went. He got Liam first, while Mary Anne and Rita talked. Rita would get her turn, but Mary Anne would be at her side. He knew he could never change that. Time healed all wounds, but he didn't have enough time left to heal the damage he'd done. He set Liam down on a blanket. He sat up, wobbled and giggled at his grandpa. Harry watched him stare around in wonder, with a world full of possibilities and promise. Unblemished. Clean.

He hoped Liam would never have to inherit his demon. Never have to taste war.

Acknowledgments

To my mother and father, who put up with my first drafts, to Les Bristol and Henry Lyman, and the rest of my family, for giving me plenty of material, to Rachel Blackbirdsong, for keeping my nose to the grindstone, to Les Edgerton and Christopher Pimental, mentors and friends, and (in no particular order) to:

Paul D. Brazill, Jack Getze, Darren Sant, David Barber, Mike Monson, Chris Rhatigan, David James Keaton, Eric Beetner, Carey Parrish, Heath Lowrance, CJ Edwards, E.A, Cook, Julie Morrigan, Absolutely Kate Pilarcik, David Siddall, Tom Pitts, Julia Madeleine, and many others...

About the Author

Liam Sweeny is an author and short story writer from the Capital District of New York. His work has been featured in print and online in places such as *Spinetingler Magazine, All Due Respect, Pulp Metal Magazine, Shotgun Honey, A Twist of Noir, Powder Burn Flash* and *The Flash Fiction Offensive.*

His early novels were science fiction/fantasy based on contemporary social issues. His detective novels, the *Jack LeClere* series, are forthcoming.

You can find out more about this author by visiting his website, www.liamsweeny.com